# HEART OF A PRICK

AN UNFORGIVABLE ROMANCE

ELLA MILES

Copyright © 2018 by Ella Miles

EllaMiles.com

Ella@ellamiles.com

Editor: Jovana Shirley, Unforeseen Editing, www.unforeseenediting.com

Cover Designer: © Cara Garrison

All rights reserved.

No part of this book may be reproduced in any form or by any electronic or mechanical means, including information storage and retrieval systems, without written permission from the author, except for the use of brief quotations in a book review.

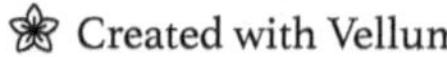 Created with Vellum

# FREE BOOKS

EllaMiles.com/freebooks

Want to get my full length romance *Not Sorry* for **free**?

Want to get my **free** bonus novella—*Aligned: Ever After?*

Want to know when I put my books on sale for **free or 99 cents**?

You can get all of the above and more goodies here:
EllaMiles.com/freebooks

# 1

## SKYE

Him, him, definitely him, not him, so hot, gross, him, him.

My mind scans all the men within eyesight as I lie on my chaise lounger by the pool at my all-inclusive resort in the Bahamas. I'm here for exactly seven days, and I plan on making the most of it. That means men. Lots and lots of men. Lots of sex. And zero thoughts about my real life, which has taken a turn for the worse recently. This week is all about relaxing and having a good time while I do it.

I take a sip of my piña colada. I've got the relaxing thing down. I have my chaise lounger, I have a bartender wrapped around my finger, bringing me drinks as soon as my glass is empty, and I'm surrounded by some of the most beautiful scenery in the world. I just need to find a man for the week, and then I'll be all set.

The problem is finding one that will fit my needs for this week. I want *wild animal* sex. The kind that involves tying each other up and spanking and all things kinky. The kind that no guy back home would dare to do.

I just don't know how to find that guy. There are plenty of

hot men at this resort. And plenty that seem single. But how do I find a guy who will give in to all my darkest desires?

"Another, Miss Skye?" my favorite bartender asks as he holds out another piña colada to me.

I grin behind my sunglasses and large hat. "Thank you, Bayron." I take the drink from him.

"You look like you're thinking hard. You shouldn't be thinking so hard. You're in paradise! You should just relax and let what happens, happen."

I nod. "Maybe. But what if I have specific needs for this trip? Needs that I'm not sure how to go about getting."

"You mean, a man?"

I nod, grinning.

He chuckles. "I don't think a woman as smart and beautiful as you should have much trouble finding a nice man."

I smirk. "But what if I don't want a nice man? What if I want a bad boy? A very, very bad boy."

He glances around at the choices currently surrounding the pool. "I don't think you should have much difficulty with that either." He winks at me.

I laugh. "You're right. But how do I choose? What if I have too many options?"

He thinks for a moment and then glances over at the small stage set up near the pool where they often have a band play music or occasionally entertain with competitions and poolside games.

"How about a competition? Winner wins a date with you."

I bite my lip as I stare at another man strutting by with muscles that contract with each step, begging to be put to use in bed with a woman like me. It could take me all week to find a man who is good in bed. But, if I can put them through a series of tests to figure out which one has the qualities I'm looking for, then I can find the guy in half the time and get on to the good stuff.

I take my hat off and push my sunglasses up on my head as I sit up on my lounger. "Let's do it!"

Bayron smiles and holds out his hand to me. I take it and let my long, dark hair with blue highlights flow down my back, matching the dark blue bikini I'm wearing. Between my hair, tattoos, and piercings in my nose, eyebrow, and ears, any man should know that I'm not looking for a good man.

Bayron leads me around the pool over to the small stage where he takes the microphone and turns it on.

"You sure about his?" he asks, whispering to me.

"Yes." I've never been so sure about needing anything. I'm desperate to find a man who can help me forget.

"Hey, Royal Bahamas Resort! Are you guys having a good time?" Bayron says.

The crowd around the pool shouts back, "Yes!"

"Awesome! I have a special treat for you today. This lovely lady here is looking for a date, and we are going to help her get one."

The crowd cheers again as I scan the pool, trying to determine which guy I want the most.

"This is Miss Skye. She's from New Mexico. She's smart and beautiful, and she's looking for a bad boy to keep her company this week. If you think you fit that bill, I want you to run onto this stage in the next ten seconds. And then the real competition will begin."

I bite my lip as the anxiety and anticipation build.

"Go! One...two...three..." Bayron starts counting, and men start running up onstage.

Some very, very good-looking men join us onstage. Men with muscles, men with beards, men with dreamy eyes, and men with tattoos. Almost all the men running up onstage look like men I'd love to take back to my room and have a test run with. But I need to choose just one. Or at least one for now.

"And time!" Bayron shouts.

He starts walking up and down the stage area, counting how many men have decided to enter. "It looks like we have fifteen men who would like to compete for a date! That's far too many." Bayron walks back to me and whispers in my ear, "What would you like them to do first?"

"Strength. I want a strong man. So, knock out the weaklings."

He nods and holds the microphone back to his lips. "Skye wants a man who's strong. So, for this competition, we are going to do as many push-ups as you can in sixty seconds. I'm going to need a little help with this one."

Bayron waves over to more of his staff to come join him. The staff line up around the men, helping them spread out around the pool area and stage.

"Everyone ready? The top ten will move on to the next round."

The men and staff nod.

"Go!" Bayron says, staring at his watch.

I watch, drooling as the men start doing push-ups as fast as they can. I can already tell by watching them which ones are truly in shape and which men aren't. And which men are too drunk to even attempt a push-up.

Two men, in particular, grab my attention. A blond man with arms for days. And a black man who is killing everyone. Both of them have excellent bodies. Either one could handle my body with ease.

"Time!" Bayron yells.

He walks down, asking the judges how many the men got.

"Okay, if you did less than a hundred, you're out!"

Five men slump back to the pool or loungers after having their egos crushed.

I look at the contestants that are left. All look fit. All look gorgeous. All look like men I'd gladly share a bed with.

Bayron again asks me what I want them to compete on next.

"I need a fast man," I answer.

He raises an eyebrow. "Skye wants a guy who is fast. I'm guessing she's still trying to weed out the in-shape guys from the ones who aren't—and she doesn't mean fast in bed. So, for our speed test, we are going to divide you into two swimming races. The fastest three in each race will move on."

I watch as the first group jumps into the water. One of the men glances over at me with hungry eyes, and my heart about stops. That's what I want. A man who desires me. I want a man who will fight and compete for me.

Bayron starts the first race, and I find myself cheering for the man who looked at me with hungry eyes. He wins easily.

The second round starts, but I find myself still entranced with the man who won the first race. I'm not even paying attention to the second race.

The winners are decided, and again, I watch as the losers sulk off, disappointed.

"What do you want me to test next, sweetheart?" Bayron asks.

"Pain."

He nods, thinking for a second. "Next, we are going to test to see who can handle pain the longest. We are going to pass out two weights to each of you, and you will hold them out to your sides, arms extended. The last six men still holding on to their weights will continue."

The weights are distributed to the six remaining men, which consists of Hungry Eyes from the swimming round, both of the men I noticed from the strength round, and three other men I haven't paid much attention to yet.

"Go!" Bayron shouts.

I watch in pain, hoping that my favorites survive to make it to the next round.

All are doing well and holding their own, but I see the blond starting to falter. He won't hold out much longer. After a few more seconds, his arms fall. Either the push-ups from earlier wore him out or he couldn't handle the pain. Either way, he's not my bad boy. Too bad.

Other men start falling, leaving me with four men. The winner of the swimming round. The winner of the strength. A new winner from the pain round. And then another man who hasn't won any but hasn't lost either.

"What's up next?" Bayron asks, jogging next to me.

"Two rounds left. The first round is dirty. Who can tell me the dirtiest, filthiest thing?"

Bayron nods. "You heard her. Prepare your best lines. We want you to get dirty. Tell her the filthiest thing you can think of."

The first man walks forward. The winner of the strength round. I want to eat up his juicy, dark muscles.

He leans down and whispers in my ear, "I want to kiss you. Claim you. Make you mine."

I smile at him as he takes a step back. It was good but not really that dirty.

Next up is the man who won the last round. He's taller than the rest, and he has deep, dark eyes. He leans down and whispers, "I want to spank your gorgeous ass while I fuck you into ecstasy."

I grin. Better.

I bite my lip while I wait for the next guy. The winner of the swimming round and my favorite so far.

He tucks a strand of my hair behind my ear, giving me goosebumps, as he says, "I want to tie you up to your bed, so you can't move. Then, I want to lick honey off your bare skin before I spank your ass until it's bright red. I won't stop until you are screaming my name, begging me to stop because you can't come anymore."

Damn. He's the clear winner so far.

Last up is a man I've barely noticed before. He says something into my ear, but I'm still so lost in the last guy's words that I don't even hear him.

"So, who is the loser?" Bayron asks.

I take a deep breath, not liking having to choose a loser.

"Number one," I say.

"Sorry, number one. You're out. We have one final round, which is..."

"Best kisser, of course," I say with a large grin as I stare at the final three men that I get to kiss.

Any one of them could be amazing in bed and give me exactly what I'm looking for this week. It all comes down to who can make my toes curl the most. And I think the man who said the dirtiest line is most likely going to be the winner.

The first man steps forward, forcefully grabs my head with both hands, and presses his lips to mine. He's aggressive. I like that. But he's so aggressive that his lips miss my mouth initially. He quickly corrects himself, pushing his tongue into my mouth like he's trying to suffocate me.

My eyes stay wide as he kisses me. I'm in shock as to what exactly he's trying to do to me. I try to grab on to him to keep from falling backward, but when he releases me, I stumble backward, unable to keep my balance.

Bayron shoots me a look, asking if I'm okay.

I nod and bite my lip to keep from giving away how horrible that kiss was, so I don't completely embarrass the poor man in front of everyone.

"All right, number two, give her your best kiss," Bayron says.

I take a deep breath to prepare myself for his kiss. I know it can't be any worse than the first. I know his kiss is going to be the best. He's won everything else. He's the one. I know it.

He walks toward me and takes me into his arms. He dips me backward as his tongue moistens his lips before he places a flawless kiss on my lips with just the tiniest hint of tongue. It is perfect. The right amount of moisture. The right amount of force. The right amount of control.

It's a pleasant kiss that warms my insides.

He brings me back up as he ends the kiss to hoots and hollers from the crowd, obviously liking the performance he put on. I liked it, too. But something was missing. Maybe it was the fact that we were in front of a large crowd. Maybe it's that I don't even know his real name, and it's keeping me from feeling more. But whatever it is, I intend on finding the missing piece to that kiss once I declare him as the winner.

I smile at him, giving him a wink, as he steps back in line with the other men.

"Woo, that was one hot kiss. I'm not sure if contestant number three can beat that, but give it your best shot," Bayron says.

I still have my eyes glued to contestant number two when contestant number three approaches.

One of his hands goes around my waist, and the other tangles in my hair as he pulls my body tightly to his, forcing me to stop looking at any other man other than him. I get one glimpse of his dark eyes before he kisses me. And then my eyes are forced closed, his body commanding that I give everything to him in the kiss. He takes his time, not rushing it, as he expertly slips his tongue into my mouth. His hand glides down from my waist to my ass as his hard cock pushes into my stomach, making it clear how badly he wants me. I feel a shock wave shoot throughout my body as he deepens the kiss, pushing me to my limit.

He stops the kiss, but I can't open my eyes yet. I'm panting heavily as he holds me in his arms. I feel his hand stroke my cheek, tucking a strand of hair behind my ear. Being so gentle after being so rough.

I open my eyes and stare into his, not sure what the hell just happened other than something amazing. It wasn't perfect. It was rough, primal, a panty-melting kind of kiss. The kind that only a bad boy with years of experience in getting dirty with plenty of women can give.

He slowly lets me go and takes his place back in line with the other men. I know that Bayron is going to ask me who the winner is. I thought it was going to be number two in a landslide. But number three just made things way more complicated. And, now, I'm not sure who I'm going to choose.

**2**

―――

**BRODY**

I STEP BACK INTO LINE, knowing that she is going to choose the guy to my left. Number two. She's had eyes only for him since the competition started. But, damn, that kiss was hot.

I've kissed strangers before but never like that. When I kissed her, she submitted to me. She wanted me to take control. Was begging for it. And I was more than happy to take it. That's what my whole life is. Taking charge and loving it.

I stare at her, commanding her to pick me with my eyes. I don't think it will work, but it's worth a shot. She's the opposite of the type of woman that I would usually go for. She's a trouble-maker; it's clear from this little game that she convinced the staff to play along with. I'm into corporate women who always dress classy with clean, sharp looks. But this woman doesn't care that she breaks all the norms when it comes to her looks. She has blue streaks in her dark hair, piercings and tattoos cover her body, and the way her body moves is like nothing I've ever seen before. She's confident and independent, but she seems tired of always being so in control of herself when it's clear from her appearance that she would rather be free, going whichever way the wind pushes her. Something is stopping her. But maybe this is her way of trying to break free of whatever is holding her back.

Behind me, I hear Noah, Harry, and Levi cheering for her to pick me. They were the ones who pushed me into this ridiculous competition in the first place. I'm here to get a break from the chaos, and I brought a few members of my team along with me. I thought they had earned a much-needed break from our daily grind at the office. They jumped at the chance to push their boss into a pissing contest over a complete stranger. I regretted bringing them the second they pushed my ass onto the stage.

Now, I'm thankful. That kiss brought me back to life again. It reminded me what taking a chance with a woman feels like and how good it feels to have a woman's lips on mine. I've taken a break from extracurricular activities, like fucking a woman, for far too long. That ends tonight. I want it to be with this woman in front of me, but if she doesn't want me, there are plenty of hot women here that I can have. I'm here for seven nights. Seven women in seven nights sounds like an excellent plan.

"Can I get a drum roll, please?" Bayron says to the crowd.

Everyone begins banging on things and shouting loudly for who they want to win.

She bites her lip—a habit of hers when she doesn't know what she wants I've noticed, or at least guess since she's done exactly that half a dozen times since the competition started. Or she does, but she is not ready to say it yet.

Her eyes are bright and wild as she looks from the first man to the second and then finally to me. I smirk at her. She won't pick me, but I want my face burned into her memory, so when she is fucking him later, my face will pop into her mind, making her second-guess her choice. I want her to regret not choosing me every day.

"And the moment of truth! Will it be contestant number

one?" Bayron says as the first guy's friends cheer him on. "Contestant number two?"

The crowd cheers loudly for contestant number two.

"Or contestant number three?"

Again, the crowd cheers loudly at the same level they did for the guy in front of me.

"And the winner is..." Bayron holds the microphone to her luscious lips, which she is still biting into.

I should have bitten her lip when I had the chance just to see what all the fuss was about.

"Number three."

The crowd cheers while I try to keep my bewilderment at winning off my face. No one needs to know that I'm not a cocky ass who thought I had this in the bag from the beginning.

The other men sulk off, disappointed that they lost. I stride forward to claim my prize and bite the lip that I've been thinking about for the last few minutes.

But Bayron stops me in my tracks before I can even get close to her.

"You hurt her, I'll kill you. And I know where you sleep at night. Understand?"

I nod, not understanding why the staff would care so much about one of its guests.

Bayron escorts me over the few feet to her.

"Skye, this is Brody. Brody, this is Skye."

"Brody?" she asks, raising an eyebrow at my name.

"Yes. You have a problem with my name?"

She laughs. "No, it sounds like a name for an arrogant man who knows how to treat a woman in bed. Just my type."

My eyes dart over her body again, taking in her breathing that has sped up as her chest rises and falls beneath the bikini top that barely covers her body. Her eyes dilate as she looks me over as well, and from how she moistens her lips, she is more than happy with what she sees me. She might have struggled with her decision between me and the other guy, but tonight, I'll make sure she forgets that any other man exists.

She licks her lips again, and I know she is preparing for another life-altering kiss. Her whole body is on alert, waiting for me to make my move now that she has chosen me. I don't know anything other than her name, but I already know from her expression that she is ready for me to sweep her off her feet and go fuck her in the nearest bedroom. I'll happily answer her wishes.

I take a step forward. I grab her and pull her close to me again. I love how her heartbeat picks up while her breathing all but stops when I simply hold her in my arms. I can't imagine what her body will do when I actually take her back to my room and strip her naked.

"Excuse me," Bayron says, pushing between us, cock-blocking me.

I glare at him like I've never glared at a man before. I won. She chose me. I played all of his stupid games. Now, let me have her.

The only thing keeping me from punching him right now is that, if I do, I know I'll get thrown out of the resort, and I won't ever be able to have her.

"The resort would like to give you both a gift," Bayron says.

"That's really not necessary, Bayron. I appreciate you playing along with my stupid game," Skye says, not looking at Bayron. She's looking at me like she's about to devour me.

My cocks twitches at that thought.

"Oh, but it is. You are one of our favorite guests, Miss Skye, and we want to make sure you are thoroughly taken care of while you are here. And that means giving you a special gift to celebrate your new relationship."

*Don't kill him. Don't kill him*, I repeat in my head. *I can't have the girl if I kill him.*

"And what gift is that?" Skye asks, her throat dry and raspy as she speaks.

"We want to make sure your first date is spectacular. So, we will go all out tonight to throw you the best first date possible. It will be the most romantic moment of your life."

"This isn't about romance," Skye says.

Bayron grabs her arm and turns her from me, whispering loud enough that I can still hear him. "A little romance never hurt anyone. I have a full day planned with a spa trip to prepare you for your date tonight." He turns his head back to me. "The date starts promptly at seven. I'll have someone send more information to your room shortly, Mr. Brody."

And then he takes Skye and walks her away from me. I don't get my kiss. I barely even got to put my hands on her. I want to run after her and kidnap her out of his pushy hands.

Skye glances back at me one last time before Bayron leads her around the building and out of view. The look she gives me is one that asks me to save her. I want to. But I know that the asshole who has a grip on her arm won't let me.

Tonight. I'll have to find a way to put an end to the romance and get to the fun part. It's clear that Skye is on the same page with me on that one.

I walk back to where the guys are still sitting.

"You won. But why do you look like you do when we are in a meeting and you hate everything that we have presented to you?" Noah asks.

"Because I'm in a foul mood."

"Where's your woman?" Harry asks, laughing.

"Bayron took her for a day of pampering before our date tonight."

"Ooh, date. I can't imagine you dating," Harry teases.

"That's because I don't date. I never have. And I don't plan on going on one tonight."

"Then, what are you going to do?"

"I'm going to kidnap the girl that I won from the bastard who thinks he's in charge of her well-being, taking back control into my own hands."

———

The seven hours until our "date" creep by slowly. The guys thought I should spend it getting drunk, which would have been the more fun way to spend the day. But I hardly ever get drunk. I don't like losing control. And, tonight, in order to get Skye away from Bayron and his staff, I need to be clearheaded.

So, instead, I spent it working out, working on my computer, and trying to get Skye out of my damn head. I've never had a woman take over my head before. Work always keeps me plenty busy enough to push away any flickers of thoughts about boobs or ass. But even work wasn't enough to keep the sway of her hips as she walked away from me out of my mind.

I hear a knock on the door to my suite. I growl, not wanting to see whoever is on the other side of that damn door unless it's Skye. The last time I answered the door, a nicely dressed man delivered my outfit for tonight. Like I was incapable of picking out my own clothes for a date.

I walk over to the door and throw it open. "What?"

Bayron frowns. "You're not wearing what was delivered to you."

I glance down at my khaki shorts and a dark V-neck T-shirt. "I'm sure I'm dressed well enough for whatever it is you are having us do."

He ignores me and pushes into my room. He walks over to the floor of my bed where I tossed the bag that was delivered to my room an hour ago. He picks it up and pulls out a light-blue button-down shirt, khaki pants, dress shoes, and a tie.

"Get dressed," he says, walking back to the door.

"And if I don't?"

"Then, I guess I'll have to find Matt, the runner-up, to take your place on the date with Skye tonight. And shave, too."

He slams the door. I rip the shirt off my body and throw it at the door, hoping it will help me not kill him. I still want to, but I try to be a good boy. I shave. I get dressed in the clothes that were delivered to me. I'll play along until I have my chance to steal Skye away to do something with a lot less romance.

I open the door when I'm dressed. Bayron scans me up and down and must approve because he waves me to follow him. I follow him out of my suite and down the hallway to the elevator.

We step on.

"So, what is this grand date you have planned for us tonight?"

"You'll find out."

"So, why are you doing this again? Trying to make tonight so perfect for us?"

The doors open to the ground floor, and we both step out.

"Because Skye is a very important guest to us."

"You mean that she is related to the owner."

He shakes his head. "No, she's just special."

"You have a thing for her or something?"

"No, Mr. Brody, I just care about her. You can ask Miss Skye why if you want more details," he says, ending the conversation.

I put my hands in my pockets as I follow him out toward the beach, waiting for a clue as to what we are doing. I find none. We stop suddenly in the sand.

"Wait here," he says.

I sigh but do what I was told.

I watch Bayron jog back up toward the resort and then disappear. I glance around me, waiting for someone to jump out and mug me if Bayron has his way. Just when I'm about done with this waiting crap, I see her.

She walks down the beach toward me without Bayron in sight—thank god. She's wearing a light-gray dress that is cut low in the front and then hugs tightly to her body before flowing around her legs. It shimmers a little toward the bottom as she walks, as if each step she takes makes the sand beneath her feet sparkle. The wind blows and tousles her hair over her head while the dress blows at her feet.

He told me to wait. Like a dog. I'm not waiting anymore.

I jog toward her far too fast for someone who is going on a date with a woman he doesn't even know. But I don't care what she thinks of me right now. Today has been hell, waiting after our kiss this morning.

She starts running toward me as well until we crash into each other, our lips locking together immediately before anyone has a chance to tell us otherwise. Our hands grab on to each other, holding us together instead of exploring each other's bodies like I really want to be doing.

Her tongue darts into my mouth, begging me to take the kiss further and making it known just how badly she has wanted to kiss me all day. It makes me hungrier. I need her now.

I deepen the kiss, pushing her lips apart wider as my tongue pushes inside her, massaging her tongue. I hear the purr in her throat in response. She loves it when I kiss her. It's what caused me to win. One kiss changed it all.

We hear a throat clearing, and she reluctantly starts to pull away, but I won't let her. Not until I've had one last taste.

I pull her bottom lip into my mouth and gently bite down. I feel her body tighten in my arms as she tries to keep the intense feelings of desire at bay.

I let her go then. Satisfied with finally getting to taste her lip.

"Right this way," Bayron says as he starts walking us down the beach.

I wrestle with myself between grabbing Skye and taking off now or waiting until later. I decide on later. I'm sure he just has a dinner or something set up. We can eat quickly and then get out of here.

Our hands interlink as we follow Bayron down the beach, still not saying a word to each other, but not needing to. We know that we want each other. In a bed. Right now.

We round the edge of the property and see a large yacht sitting at the end of the pier.

"Your date awaits," Bayron says, pointing toward the boat.

My mouth drops open. I know how much a yacht like that costs. There is no way that this is our gift from the resort. Even if we only go out for an hour, it would cost them more than both of our rooms for the entire week, combined.

"You're kidding, right?" I ask.

Bayron smiles. "Only the best for Miss Skye."

He starts walking down the long wooden peer. The yacht gets larger and larger with each step we take.

"He's joking, right? If this is really our gift, you know they are going to expect us to pay them back somehow," I lean over and say to Skye.

She shrugs. "Let's just get the romance over with, so we can move on to the fun part." She winks.

I squeeze her hand tighter. "Done."

We keep walking toward the yacht, and the boy part of me that still gets excited about shiny things with fast motors and expensive boats gets me far too giddy as we stop in front of it. I've never been on a yacht before, and all I want to do is go explore every inch of it. Talk to the captain about how it works, how expensive it is, and how fast it can go.

But then I look over at Skye, and I forget about the damn

yacht. We could be riding a bus for all I care as long as I get to hold her again. Kiss her. Fuck her. Nothing else matters. Not even figuring out the crazy reason we are getting to ride in this yacht instead of just getting a romantic dinner on the beach, like every other couple who stays at this resort.

Bayron holds his hand out to Skye. She lets go of my hand and takes his as he helps her into the yacht.

I grind my teeth to keep from chewing Bayron out for taking Skye from me for a single second. I really need to get my anger in check. Bayron is just doing his job. He's not hitting on Skye. And it's clear Skye is only interested in me. But I can't. I've never felt such claim over a woman before, especially one that I've only ever kissed.

I climb up onto the yacht behind Skye.

"Have a good date. If you need anything, just ask one of the wait staff on board or the captain."

I turn back to look at Bayron. "How long are we going to be on the yacht?" I'm starting to think that he's going to trap me on this boat so that I can't escape and am forced to be romantic with Skye.

He smiles. "Are you well taken care of, Miss Skye?"

She gives me a sideways glance with a sparkle in her eyes before she takes my hand again. "I think I'm in very good hands."

"How long?" I ask again, not about to be trapped on this yacht for my entire vacation.

"Don't worry, Mr. Brody; there are beds on the yacht," he says with a wink.

The yacht starts moving gently away from the pier. I could jump back onto the pier. But I don't think I could get Skye to come with me. I hate not having control. I hate not knowing where we are going or when we are coming back. But, until this yacht turns around, I'm going to have to find a way to let all of that go.

"Come on," Skye says, pulling me toward the front of the yacht as we head out into the ocean, toward the sun that is just beginning to set.

We stop at the railing at the front of the boat, still gripping on to each other's hands while resting them on the railing. We stand in silence just staring at the ocean.

"I'm sorry," Skye says as she looks out at the ocean.

"Why are you sorry?"

"For Bayron. He means well, but sometimes, he takes things too far. You never agreed to being kidnapped on a boat with me."

My eyes widen a little at just how on the nose she is about my feelings. But, as soon as she says it out loud, I realize how absolutely ridiculous my feelings are.

I stroke her cheek. "Don't be sorry. For any of it. There are worse ways I could be spending my time than trapped on a boat with a beautiful woman like you."

She blushes a little. "Let's try to survive for a couple of hours, and then we can have them turn it around."

I arch an eyebrow. "You can have them turn the yacht around at any time, and they'll listen to you?"

Skye turns toward me with an amused smile. "You really thought they were kidnapping us and holding us hostage until we had the romantic date that they wanted, didn't you?"

I shrug. "Bayron came to my room, forced me to wear this outfit, and then escorted me down to the beach where he told me to stay. Then, he forced me onto a boat, and I have no idea how long I will be on it. Seems like kidnapping to me."

She places her hand on my chest, running it over the smooth fabric, feeling the muscles that ripple beneath her hand. "You're right. This shirt is horrible." She winks at me. "And I'll let you repay the favor by kidnapping me anytime." Her hand dances across my chest as she looks to her right. "It looks like dinner is ready." She sighs.

I look to my left and see three waiters with a fancy table with a white tablecloth and red roses everywhere. This is going to be the most romantic date of my life in the most romantic of places. This is meant to be the start of an epic love story. It's just not the love story that either of us wants.

I walk over to the table and pull out the chair like the gentleman that I am for Skye to sit.

She shakes her head and walks over to the other chair. She pulls it out herself and takes a seat.

I rub the back of my neck, completely bewildered by this woman.

"This isn't a date. Take a seat, Romeo," she says, pointing at the chair that I just pulled out for her.

I take a seat. "I thought that was exactly what this was. A date."

"What do you want to drink?" she asks me.

"Wine."

"No, not wine. What else do you want?"

"Bourbon."

She looks at the waiters. "Bring us a bottle of bourbon and tequila and two glasses. Then, leave us alone until we call for you."

The waiters nod and then leave to I assume follow her instructions.

"Why can't we have wine?" I ask.

"Because wine is for people on a date."

"And we aren't on a date?" I ask, still not understanding what we are doing then.

"Exactly. We aren't on a date." She reaches into the middle of the table, grabbing the red roses sitting on the table. "Get the petals," she commands.

I quickly sweep the flower petals into my hand, not sure what we are doing with them. Two waiters return with the bottles and glasses.

"Set them on the table in the center," Skye commands.

They do without hesitation or blink of the eye.

"Now, take these, and leave us alone. We will come inside to grab food later." Skye holds out the flowers, and I do the same. The waiters take the flowers and petals and leave us alone.

Skye grabs the tequila bottle and glass and pours herself a glass almost completely full with way more tequila than what she should be drinking. She takes a swig as she leans back in the chair until the front legs are off the ground. "Better. Now, it's not a date."

I nod as I look around at the yacht. She might have taken away the flowers and the wine, but we are still on a boat with gold-colored edging and dark wood floors, which costs more than quadruple the price of most people's houses. We are still alone on a yacht in the middle of the ocean with the sun setting before us. Getting rid of a few flowers doesn't get rid of the fact that this is definitely a date.

"Now, you just need to get rid of the sunset and start burping or something so that I stop thinking of you as this beautiful woman I want to fuck."

She burps.

I laugh.

"I can't do anything about the sunset. And I want you to want to fuck me, just not date me."

I grab the bottle of bourbon and pour myself a reasonable glass.

"So, what are we doing if we aren't on a date?"

"We are negotiating."

I take a drink of my bourbon. "And what are we negotiating?"

"What I want from you."

She takes another drink of her tequila, emptying almost half of the glass, before she leans forward, the front legs of her chair touching back down on the ground. She harshly places the glass back on the table, and she folds her arms in front of her.

"Here are my terms. I want one week of filthy, dirty, *tie me up, spank me till I come*, dangerous sex. I want the kind of sex that makes me forget about everything. I want the kind that makes me feel alive again. The kind you only read about in naughty romance books or when watching porn. That's what I want. Can you give me that, Brody?"

Her eyes are dark and serious when she talks. Her voice is stern and unwavering. Something happened to her to make her need this or at least think that this is what she wants. And I don't care to know what it is. I don't want to get involved in her clearly messy life.

I lean forward on the table so that I'm eye-to-eye with her. "I can make your darkest fantasies come true."

She grins. "Good. I chose my man well then."

I nod.

"Now, the terms. You are mine for the week. You don't get to go around, fucking other women and then fuck me. I'll have sex with you as much as you want this week, but I'm not willing to share."

I smirk. "I don't share either."

"Good. I also don't do attachment. We aren't dating. We aren't a couple. This goes nowhere after this week."

"I don't date, so it won't be a problem—as long as you can keep your emotions out of this." I eye her with suspicion.

She growls. "Just because I'm a woman doesn't mean I have

emotions that need more controlling than you do. When I look at you, I feel nothing but the need to rip your clothes off."

I narrow my eyes, searching hers for a bit of untruth. I find none.

"Satisfied?" she asks.

"Yes."

"Lastly, we don't discuss anything personal. We don't talk about what our jobs are or where we live. We don't do last names. You don't introduce me to your friends. I don't hear about your past girlfriends, and you don't ask about my past lovers. We learn nothing about each other, except how you like to fuck me and what each other sounds like when we come. That's it."

"I couldn't agree more."

"Do you have any terms or requests?"

"Just one. That you remember the word *red.* It's your safe word when you can't handle the pain or the sex anymore, and you are going to need to use it."

Her eyes deepen, and her lips curl up just a little at that thought.

"I don't think there is anything you can do to make me use that word. But I'll remember."

My eyes scan hers. She's been hurt. Really, really hurt. She wants me to take away her pain with more pain and sex. She's right that it will help her for the week. I'm just glad I won't be there when she goes back to her normal life and has to deal with whatever crap she is hiding from me.

"Food or sex first?" she asks.

I smirk. "I forgot one final rule. You want BDSM, right? You want me to tie you up, spank you, whip you—the whole package, right?"

She nods, her mouth open and panting.

"Then, you have to give up control. You do exactly what I say, when I say it. You don't get to say no to anything. You just do without thinking. If it's too much, you tell me *red* to stop. Otherwise, you don't think for the rest of the week."

"Exactly."

My inner demon comes out the second she says that. She just gave me complete control over her body. And I plan on taking advantage of having that control.

"Excuse me," one of the waiters says.

I exhale deeply. I'm pretty sure steam blows out of my ears from my pent-up anger with Bayron, but it is now getting directed at this new man who I won't let cockblock me. Not now that I finally get her with no strings attached.

Skye gives the man an equally perturbed look. "What?" she snaps.

"I'm very sorry to interrupt you, but the captain's cat we think is having a seizure or something. We can either turn back or you can—"

Skye sighs, getting up from the table, looking me dead in the eye. Then, she breaks her own rule, telling me something about herself. "I'll take a look at the cat."

## 3

## SKYE

*Damn it!*

All I wanted to do was have some filthy, dirty, mind-blowing sex with a hot stranger who wants the same thing that I do. How hard is that to get? Between Bayron forcing me into this date and now the captain's cat, I'm not sure if I will ever get what I want.

I quickly follow the waiter back to the captain's quarters where they have the cat lying on a bed. I try not to think about how many rules I'm breaking by showing Brody that I'm a vet. I just want to take care of the cat and then get back to the part where Brody fucks me. The cat is probably fine anyway.

But, when I put my hands on the cat, I know that the cat isn't fine. He needs help. *Immediately.*

"Get me the first aid kit. Now," I say calmly, looking at the waiter.

"Is he going to be okay?" the captain asks.

"I need you to get me towels, his food, and favorite toys. Understand?"

He nods.

"Go," I say sternly, just trying to get him out of the room, so I can do what I need to do. I don't need any of the things I just asked him to get.

The waiter returns with the first aid kit and puts it on the bed. The cat isn't breathing. I quickly look in his mouth to see if anything is obstructing his airflow. I can't see anything, but most likely, there is something, and I just can't see it. If he was having a seizure before, he might have thrown something up that is now lodged in his throat.

I start performing CPR, but air isn't getting into his lungs like I expected.

"Are you squeamish?" I ask the waiter as I throw open the first aid kit, hoping it has everything I need.

"Yes."

"Then, get out."

It has a scalpel and gauze. "I need a straw," I say, glancing around the room.

"Here," Brody says, handing me a straw as he kneels down next to me on the bed.

I give him a wide-eyed stare. I don't have time to ask how or where he found it.

"I'm not squeamish," he says.

I nod, not having time to deal with if he is or isn't. I have a cat to save.

"Start opening those gauze packets."

He does while I grab the scalpel. I don't have time to shave the cat like I'd like or give the cat anything for pain. Instead, I palpate and then make a quick and exact cut into the cat's lungs.

I grab the straw and carefully place it into the opening. I grab the gauze from Brody to stop the bleeding.

"Come on," I say, waiting for oxygen to get into the cat's lungs.

His lungs slowly start filling and then emptying with air, and I let out a deep breath.

"Hold him still," I tell Brody.

His hands hold the cat that will start feeling more alive now that he is getting oxygen.

"Do you have your phone on you?"

Brody pulls out his phone and hands it to me. I turn the flashlight on and open the cat's mouth to get a better look while I take the tweezers. It takes me several minutes to find the obstruction, but I finally find the piece of plastic that is lodged in his throat. I pull it out, and then slowly, the cat starts breathing on his own.

"Good kitty," I say, petting his head. I wait a few more minutes to make sure he is breathing well on his own before I take the straw out and cover the small wound with gauze and wrap.

The captain runs back into the room. "I couldn't find his favorite toys."

I smile. "It's okay. Your cat is doing much better now. You should have your vet take a look at him tomorrow to make sure he's still doing okay, but he's in the clear."

I can see the relief all over the man's face. It's one of the best parts of the job—watching owners realize that their beloved pet is going to be all right.

He runs over to the cat and wraps his arms around him while I take a step back.

I don't dare glance over at Brody. I don't want to know what he's thinking. We were supposed to remain a mystery to each other. That was how we would be able to remain unattached. But, in a matter of seconds, I destroyed all of that.

I walk out of the room, knowing that Brody is following. I walk back to the front of the boat as the first part of darkness starts covering the sky. I walk back to the railing to look out as the stars begin to take over the sky.

Brody slowly walks over next to me. He doesn't touch me. He

just leans on the railing and looks out at the ocean and sky with me.

"I wish I could pretend like I didn't just see that, but I'm not a very good actor."

I sigh. "It's okay. It was stupid to think that we could spend a week together and not learn some basic facts about each other." I turn toward Brody. "I'm a veterinarian, if you didn't figure that out already. I like animals more than I like people. And, if you think what I did back there was impressive, don't. I don't want you thinking I'm this amazing human being you should date after this. I'm not that good of a person. If that had been a human back there, I would have let them die. This changes nothing."

He smirks.

"What's so amusing?"

"You are the strangest human being I've ever met."

My lips slowly curl up. "You think I'm strange. Good."

I walk back to the table, pour us each another drink, and then walk back to the railing, handing Brody his drink.

"So, tell me something about yourself since you now know too much about me."

Brody takes a slow sip of his drink as he stares deeply into my eyes. "You don't want me to tell you anything about myself."

"Yes, I do."

"No, you don't."

"Yes, it's only fair."

He grabs my hand and roughly pulls me to him. He's done that a couple of times now. And, every single time, it shocks and excites me. My body comes alive with a fire that I don't know how to extinguish and don't really want to get rid of. I want more and more of his body. I want to feel and see every glorious inch of his hardness that he teases me with but hasn't shown me enough of yet.

He looks at me like he wants to devour me.

My body screams back, *Yes, yes, yes. Kiss me. Devour me. Do whatever dirty things you think of in your mind but haven't dared to do yet. I need it. I want it. I can't live without it.*

"My favorite movie is *The Lord of the Rings*."

My head snaps back as I look at him incredulously. I was expecting a kiss; instead, I got a lousy fact about him.

"If you are going to share something about yourself, you could at least share something interesting. Your favorite movie doesn't count."

"I just told you one of the most important things about myself."

"No, you told me a random trivia fact. What your favorite movie is tells me nothing about you."

He pulls me tighter, and I try to keep my body from getting too excited because, apparently, we are going to argue about what makes a trivia fact worth caring about. And, after we are done with that, I'm sure we will be interrupted again by the staff to handle another crisis, and we will never actually have sex. But my body doesn't care about any of that. My body thinks that, anytime our bodies are within three feet of each other, we are about to have sex.

"Actually, it tells you everything."

"How?" I ask, breathing heavily.

"Well, if I had said my favorite movie was *Die Hard* or *The Godfather*, what would you have thought?"

"That you are like every other hot-blooded male on this planet, who can't think for themselves."

He nods. "Exactly."

His hand tangles in my hair, and I can't think anymore about anything other than his hand.

"So, what does me liking *The Lord of the Rings* tell you about me?"

"Um..." I can't think. *Why can't he tell that, when he touches me, I can't think at all?*

He smirks, and his damn dimples catch my attention now as my mouth goes dry. I glance up at his eyes that are laughing at my predicament. He knows. He knows exactly what he is doing to me. He's teasing me while trying to have a stupid conversation. But I don't want to be teased. I want to be fucked.

I can play this game.

I take a drink of my tequila as I take a step back. I toss my hair over my head, forcing him to let go of my hair as I expose my bare neck to him. His eyes deepen, and he clears his throat as he stares at me.

"It tells me that you are a nerd who likes watching people fight over a ring."

He frowns and takes a step toward me. "No, it tells you that I'm an intelligent man who has a dark imagination and isn't afraid to go after what he wants."

It's my turn to swallow hard. I watch him watch my throat as he thinks about what dirty thing he is going to do to me.

"Fuck me before some other crazy thing happens that stops us," I say.

Before he can respond, a loud popping sound makes us both jump. We turn out toward the ocean where the sound is coming from.

Fireworks.

He arches an eyebrow at me.

"Yes, Bayron planned the fireworks for us," I say, groaning.

It's beautiful and romantic, and it would be perfect if I were actually on a date with a man I thought was capable of dating when I got home. But that's not what this is.

I don't want to watch the fireworks. But the resort spent far too much money on them for us not to watch. So, I lean over the railing, hoping that the show ends soon.

Brody walks behind me, wrapping his arms around me as his body presses against my back.

"We should watch, but it doesn't mean that you need to make this any more romantic than it already is," I hiss.

His mouth moves to my ear. "Don't react; the staff is watching."

"What?" And then his hand slips into the front of my dress, grabbing my breast.

I gasp.

"Don't react," he commands with a growl to his voice.

I suck in a breath as I feel an ice cube dance over my nipple. His mouth lightly kisses my exposed neck, and the combination sends chills shooting through my body.

"You've wanted me to kiss your neck all night."

"Yes," I whisper.

"I've wanted to do this all night." He hikes my dress up, and his hand slips into my panties.

I groan as his fingers slip inside my drenched pussy.

"Not. A. Sound," he says.

I bite my lip to keep from screaming. I don't know why it matters if I moan a little. The fireworks would more than cover up any sound I made.

His fingers slide in and out of me, and my hips start buckling as he moves.

"Don't move, sweetheart, or I'll stop." His voice is serious and threatening.

I don't know how not to move. I don't know how not to make a sound. But I'm so desperate to get fucked by him that I'll do anything I can to give in to his demands. I grab the railing hard, forcing myself to remain still, as I continue to bite my lip.

His fingers slip back out of me, and for a second, all I feel is his heavy breathing on my neck. He kicks my legs apart a little more, and then his cock enters me without warning.

I bite my lip hard, causing it to bleed to keep from screaming.

"Good girl," he whispers into my ear when I do everything I can to follow his command.

I don't know if he has a condom on or not. I don't know if the entire staff can see us right now or not. But neither matters. My body is his. He can do whatever he wants to it. I instantly trust him. And the way he controls my body shows me just how correct I was in giving him that power.

"Aw, baby, I can already feel your pussy starting to tighten around my cock."

I pant, unable to bite down on my lip any longer.

"You want to come so badly."

"Yes."

"But you don't get to come. Not yet. You're not ready."

I swallow, trying to push down my orgasm that I'm on the edge of having.

"I can't."

"Don't come, Skye," he commands as he fucks me, making it almost impossible for me not to.

I try to hold on to his words. I try to do exactly what he says when every part of my body is begging me to do the opposite. I need to come. My body won't let me hold back much longer.

He grabs on to my hips as he pushes his thick, long cock into me harder, driving me so close to the edge that I'm not sure there is anything that can keep me from coming.

"No, Skye," he warns.

I stop. I don't know how his words are able to control me despite his body pushing me to do the opposite. But my body listens. At least, one more time.

"You want to come, Skye?"

"Yes."

"You think you've earned it?"

"Yes."

He snickers. "You think this was hard, but you don't know how bad I can be."

I suck in a breath, trying desperately to hold on as he continues to thrust harder, making the task impossible.

"Come."

One tiny word, and my body responds. My pussy tightens around his cock as my body explodes more fiercely than the fireworks still shooting off in front of us. I don't know if I'm still supposed to be quiet or not, but I can't be quiet. I open my mouth to moan, and his mouth captures mine. I moan into his mouth instead of screaming into the night.

I don't know if he comes. I don't notice the fireworks. I don't notice if anyone is watching us. All I can do is come over and over until my body finally stills.

I'm a strong woman. I work out daily. But I have no strength left. I collapse into his arms, unable to even stand.

He grins like the asshole he is.

"I think I chose correctly," I say, trying to catch my breath and strength.

He tucks his cock back into his pants before he scoops me up into his arms. "I didn't do my job very well if you are still thinking about other men."

My head rests against his hard chest. I want him to get naked in one of the bedrooms. I want to do that again and again, but I can barely move.

"I'm not thinking of them."

He smirks. "I know."

He carries me inside and down a hallway, stopping outside a door that has our names written on it in hearts.

"What did Bayron think? That he would put our name on a couple of hearts, and by the end of the date, I would be proposing to you?" he asks as he pushes the door open.

We both stare at the bed that is covered in rose petals and has two swan towels kissing. There is a bottle of champagne chilling with chocolate-covered strawberries sitting on the table next to the bed.

I sigh. "I think that is exactly what Bayron was thinking."

"I don't want to put you on the bed."

"Why? You think I'll catch romantic fever if you let me near some rose petals?"

"No, I think we are both going to fall asleep before I get to fuck you again."

He looks down at me, and I see the lust that I feel reflecting in his eyes.

"But, if I put you down anywhere else, I'm afraid you will collapse from exhaustion."

I laugh. "Whose fault is that?"

"Fine. I'll let you sleep well tonight, but you'd better get plenty of rest because, tomorrow, I plan on making up for lost time."

I bite my lip, liking that thought. "Deal."

He tosses me onto the bed and climbs into bed next to me.

"You're not going to undress?" I ask, disappointed.

"If I undress either of us, I'm going to fuck you again. And, since you trusted me with your body, I know I need to pace ourselves so that I can have a full day with you tomorrow."

I sigh. "Fine."

His arms wrap around me, and I snuggle against his body. I'm not sure if snuggling breaks the rules of getting too close or doing anything other than sex, but right now, I'm too tired to think about it.

"Why did you pick me instead of the dickhead?" he asks.

My eyes open, and I turn. "Why does it matter?"

"Because I'm a man, and I need to know that I blew away my competition."

I laugh. "Sorry, the competition was close. I chose you because you kissed better."

"Not because of the naughty things I said?"

I blush. I don't want to tell him that I was so caught up with the other guy that I didn't even hear what he said.

He shakes his head. "That's what I thought. You didn't even hear what I said, did you?"

I blush a deeper shade of red. "No."

He growls, "Well then, you missed out."

"What did you say?"

"I guess you'll have to find out tomorrow."

I sigh. "Tell me."

"I'll show you later. Now, sleep, and if you dream about dick-face or even think about him again, I'll punish you."

He pulls me close against his body, and I close my eyes. He thinks I thought of another guy for even a second after he fucked me. That's his goal—to eliminate any thoughts of any other man from my brain. He just doesn't realize that he's already done it.

He's fucked me once, and my body already belongs to him. I can't remember any other man ever fucking me. And, as much as I want to sleep, all I can think about is forcing my brain to try to remember what dirty, filthy thing he said to me so that I can figure out what naughty thing he has planned for me tomorrow.

## 4

## BRODY

*Why the fuck did I bring up dickface?*

Because I'm a jealous asshole who can't tolerate her thinking about any man other than me. I needed to hear her say that she was mine. Because I'm a controlling fucker who wants complete control over her body.

I'm already close to controlling her body. Her body followed almost every command. I could have made her come anytime after my cock entered her pussy. She would have done anything I wanted. But she still tried to scream. That was the only command she couldn't completely follow.

One fuck, and I already own her body. But my dark heart wants to control more than just her body. I want to control everything about her. Her every movement. Her every breath. Who she talks to. What she does. What she thinks.

I've gotten one tiny taste of what controlling her would be like, and now, my thoughts have turned into an asshole. Only a giant prick would want this much control over another person.

I thought I came here to get away from the control that I was used to at home. But, instead, I came here and got more control over another person than I'd ever thought they would give me. I got a taste of what I'd always wanted but never thought I could have. And, now, I want more.

She stirs in my arms. She's been out since about five minutes after her head hit the pillow. Yesterday was exhausting for her. But today is going to be much worse. I have too many dirty thoughts playing in my head that I need to experience with her. We only have a week together. And I plan on making the most of it by playing out every dark fantasy that either of us has ever had.

She grins when she sees me.

"Sleep well?" I ask, already knowing the answer.

She stretches her arms over her head. "Yes."

"Good. Now, get off my arm. You've been lying on it all night."

She rolls off my arm with a giggle. "You're not serious, right? I haven't actually been lying on your arm all night."

I rub my arm, trying to get the feeling back into it. "I'm dead serious."

"You could have just moved me."

"But then you might have woken up."

She narrows her eyes as she tucks her hair behind her ear. "We should probably get going. I want to get out of this dress, and the staff would probably like time to clean before their next excursion."

She walks out of the bedroom without giving me a chance to respond. I follow her, hating that she is making a decision without me. I wanted her one more time on the yacht first, but by the time I chase after her, she is already thanking the crew and exiting the boat.

I run after her. "What are you doing?"

She turns and looks at me, still staring at me with her big eyes. "Exactly what I said. Getting off the boat and going back to my room to shower and get ready for the day."

I frown. "I'm the one in control this week. You do what I say. You don't get to make decisions anymore."

Her eyes brighten in amusement. "No, you get control over my body when we are having sex. We aren't fucking right now, so that means I have control over my own decisions. Understand? If not, I'll find a new man."

I take a step toward her and tower over her. "You wouldn't find a new man. You want my cock, not anyone else's. And, as far as our agreement, fine. I control your body when we are fucking, nothing more."

"Thank you. Now, I'm going to go up to my room to shower and put my swimsuit on. Meet me in my room in twenty."

I nod and watch her walk off to go change. I agree because it's what I want. I want her in her swimsuit. I want to fuck her again, but just because I want to fuck her doesn't mean we have to stay in the bedroom.

———

The door to her suite opens, and my jaw drops for more than one reason. The swimsuit that she is wearing is racy as hell. It's white and simple, but that is where the innocence of it ends. The front barely covers her breasts, and her nipples push hard against the fabric into peaks that I'm desperate to suck.

"Come in," she says, turning, and that's when I get the view of her ass in a thong bikini.

Goddamn, her body is amazing. It's clear that she works out regularly, and whatever she is doing, it's working. Really, really working. The muscles in her legs and ass draw me in and make me think of a few too many crazy positions to try. I know last night took a lot out of her, but it wasn't because her body couldn't handle it. It was more like her mind wasn't prepared for it. It makes my naughty plans for today that much more exciting.

And then I get a view of her suite, and my jaw drops again. She either is the highest-priced veterinarian in the country to be able to afford a suite like this or she has other money. The suite is three times the size of mine. I thought mine was outrageous and one of the best suites, but clearly, I was wrong. She has her own private pool in her room along with two hot tubs, an amazing view of the ocean, a living room, a dining room, and it looks like at least two or three bedrooms that jet off from the main room.

"What do you think of my swimsuit?" Skye asks, flaunting her body in front of me as she puts sunglasses on her head.

I growl.

She laughs. "That was the answer I was hoping for."

I bite my lip to keep from asking my questions about how she makes this kind of money. We promised we wouldn't share anything personal about each other, but now that I've seen her room, I have a better understanding of why we got the yacht yesterday. The resort didn't pay for it. She did. Either through her payments on this room or separately, it doesn't matter. She paid for it.

"Want to go to the beach or stay here and do something naughty?" she asks as she bends over, flashing me a view of her plump, tight ass.

I want her. But I can't have her here. Not right now. My ego can't handle it. Not until I figure out how she has this much money. I need to know if she earned it or if she has a rich daddy or something that is paying for all of this.

"Both."

Her eyes light up.

I walk over to the bag she has been packing for the beach and pick it up, throwing it over my shoulder before I take her hand.

She gives me a disappointed look. But I don't let it stop me. I lead her out until I find a private spot on the beach with two lounge chairs and an umbrella. I dig her towel out of the bag and put it on one of the chairs.

"I'll go get you a drink. What do you want?"

She frowns. "You don't need to get me a drink. A bartender will be around in a few minutes."

"No need to wait. I'll get you something now. Do you just want whatever the drink of the day is or a piña colada or what?"

"Drink of the day is fine," she says.

I expect her to smile or give me some indication that she is happy that I'm doing something nice for her. Instead, I get a blank expression. I walk away up the beach and toward the bar that sits on the edge of the property.

I pull out my phone as I walk and type in everything that I know about her, which isn't much. Her first name and that she's a veterinarian. And then I hope that something comes up.

I take a seat on one of the small circular barstools attached to the bar.

"Can I get two drinks of the day?" I ask while I wait for my Wi-Fi connection to kick in and pull up the results.

The bartender nods and begins making our drinks.

Slowly, the search results start coming up. I click on the first article and watch as her big eyes and sly lips come up on the screen. The only difference between her now and in this picture is that her hair was red then and, now, it's blue. I didn't expect to find out much about her so quickly without even a last name to go off of. I glance to the two other people in the image next to her and read the caption. But I guess, when you are friends with a princess and prince, Google assumes you are searching for that famous Skye and not someone else.

I continue reading through the article but don't find out much more about her. I search through other articles, but all I can find out about Skye is her connection to her princess best friend. I don't find anything about a rich father or that she sold a company that made her millions. She has a rich friend. That must be why she is treated like royalty when she comes here even though she isn't a princess herself; she knows a princess.

I close my phone as the bartender hands me our drinks.

"Thanks," I say, taking the drinks and walking back to Skye.

My ego feels less crushed, knowing that she doesn't make outrageous amounts of money; she just has a rich friend who takes care of her.

"Here you go," I say, holding her drink out to her.

"Thanks," she says, forcing a fake smile onto her lips.

She sits on her lounge chair, half in and half out of the sun.

"Do you want me to move the umbrella, so you are out of the sun? Or do you want to work on your tan?" I ask.

"I'm fine as is."

I take a seat in the lounge chair next to her, and we both stare out at the ocean while drinking our drinks. I'll give her a few minutes just to enjoy the beach before I make my move. It's a quarter till eleven. I'll start my plan on the hour. It will make it easier for me to execute.

She eyes me out of the corner of her eye as she drinks, but she doesn't say anything. She just drinks, like I'm not even here, obviously lost in thought.

I take her hand and gently kiss it.

"What are you doing?" she asks, her voice exploding with her anger toward me, which she has obviously been hiding all morning.

"Kissing your hand," I say, confused as to why she is so upset.

She pulls her hand away and sits up, straddling the lounge chair. "No, what are you doing, being so nice to me? The opening doors for me and carrying my bag and fetching me drinks and, now, kissing my hand. It has to stop!"

I wrinkle my forehead because I think she has absolutely lost it. "I can't do nice things for you? Why?"

"Because that's not what we are. We aren't boyfriend and girlfriend. We aren't dating. We aren't doing anything with emotions. We are just fucking. The rougher, the better. So, stop being so nice to me."

I laugh. I can't help it. "I can't be nice to you? Seriously? I get that you want the bad boy in the bedroom, but what I've done so far isn't even that nice. I got you a drink and carried your bag. So what? Next time we need a drink, you can go get it if it will make you feel better."

"It will."

"Fine." I slurp down the rest of my drink. "Then, get me a refill."

She smirks and storms off toward the bar to get us new drinks while I try to figure out what the hell just happened. She's an independent firecracker. I know that. I just didn't realize that doing anything for her would turn into such a fight. There is something I'm missing. I know that. I just don't know what it is or if it matters.

I have six days left with her. I just have to let more of my asshole nature out so that she doesn't feel like I want something after the six days are up. I don't. And not trying is easy. I'll just pretend like she doesn't exist, except when I want sex from her.

"Here," she says, roughly handing me my drink.

I take the drink from her without saying thank you, without a grin, without anything.

She carefully watches me as she takes a seat next to me. "You're not living up to your end of the deal."

I exhale deeply, closing my eyes and leaning back. "How am I not living up to the deal?"

"You're supposed to be giving me hot, *I can't move for a week* sex. Not lying around, giving me compliments, and getting me drinks."

I don't open my eyes. "Seven minutes."

"What?"

"I'm giving you *I can't move for a week* sex starting in seven minutes."

"Why seven minutes?"

"If you had listened to me instead of your favorite to win yesterday, then maybe you would know the answer to that."

She sighs while I grin on the inside. She's flustered and confused. She says that she wants me to be in control, to be an ass, but when I do it for even a second, she hates it.

I hear her shift in her seat, not able to get comfortable while she waits for what's going to happen in seven minutes. I listen to her breathing get faster and faster. She sighs every few seconds, annoyed that she gave up control to me and this is how I use it. To torture her. She slurps from her drink, trying to calm her mind. But it won't work either. She wants me too badly.

I, on the other hand, have never been more relaxed.

"It's been seven minutes," she says, her face right over mine as she waits for me to open my eyes.

"Six minutes. It's been six minutes."

"How do you know that? Your eyes have been closed the entire time."

"I know because you are far too restless to wait the entire seven minutes, so that means that only six minutes must have passed."

I open my eyes, and she bites her lip as trying to keep it from curling up in a smile.

"What happened to you giving me complete control?"

She narrows her eyes as she tucks her hair behind her ear while she still hovers over me. "I've realized that I'm not very good at it."

"No, you're not. But you're going to be."

I tackle her back onto her lounge chair, and she gasps. I pin her body beneath me. With my eyes, I make my intentions clear of exactly what I want to do with her.

"No, we can't," she says, looking around at the other people on the beach.

"We are."

"Brody, we can't—"

My mouth presses down on her soft lips, which are trembling as she has thoughts of getting caught having sex on the beach. She thinks she has a choice, but she doesn't. If she wants me to continue to fuck her for the rest of the week, then she has to do exactly what I say.

"Fuck me right here. Anyone could see us. We could get kicked off the resort for this. Arrested even. But none of that matters because you can't help but fuck me," I say into her lips as I continue kissing her.

She writhes beneath me, trying to fight between what she wants and what she feels is right.

My hand slips down between her legs, beneath her bikini bottoms. I rub over her clit and then into her pussy. She wants me. Now. She can't hide what her body is telling me.

"Decide, Skye. Fuck me here, or don't fuck me ever again."

Her eyes search mine. "You couldn't stop fucking me if I didn't fuck you here."

I smirk. "There are plenty of other women I could fuck. You said you wanted a bad boy, a man to take charge and play out your wildest fantasies. So, either let me have the control or find someone else."

"Fuck me," she says without hesitation. Whatever doubts she had before are gone. She wants me, and that's all that matters to her now.

"Good girl," I say, settling between her legs as I bite her bottom lip hard for hesitating in the first place.

She whimpers at the sting of the pain, but it does want I intended it to do. It makes me the sole focus of her attention. She's forgotten that we are on a beach chair, only feet from the nearest couple.

I move my kisses down her neck, and my fingers trace circles between her folds. Her breathing is slow and heavy, but I know it's soon going to turn fast and desperate.

"Grab my cock," I say into her ear.

Her hand finds the waistband of my swim trunks, and she slips her hand inside, finding my hard cock, stroking it over and over.

"That's my girl," I say, loving how she strokes my cock with just the right amount of pressure.

I pull a condom out of my pocket and place it in her other hand.

"Put it on," I command.

Her eyes grow heavy as she rips the condom wrapper open with her teeth.

"Don't move," I say as a couple walks by us, hand in hand.

I can feel her heart racing in her chest. She holds her breath, not moving an inch. And I'm afraid she's going to back out and not let me fuck her.

The couple passes, and I look her in the eye again, trying to get her focus back on me. "Put the condom on."

She takes a deep breath with a sexy grin. "Don't worry, handsome." She leans forward, firmly kissing me as her tongue darts into my mouth. "I don't think I could ever stop fucking you."

I growl and shove her hand holding the condom toward my cock, needing the damn condom on now before I fuck her whether it's on or not.

She gets the hint and places the condom on. I shove her

bikini bottoms down and pull my cock out, not caring who is looking as I slide it into her slit. Her hands tangle in my hair, pulling me closer to her, and I push harder inside her.

I know I need to make this fast, but I could stay buried deep inside her forever if she let me. And I have a feeling, from the look of ecstasy on her face, that she would.

But I can hear people coming. I know that our risky moment can only be that—just a moment. That, if I want to fuck her properly, I'm going to need to find a place more private than the beach. Because, if we get caught, I'll lose her trust and ability to take control of her body. And I won't give that up.

So, I fuck her hard. Fast. Thrusting quickly without giving her a second to breathe.

"Come, Skye," I command as I come deep inside her, not waiting for her.

She comes as she buries her face into my shoulder to keep from crying out.

"Hey, guys! Look, I found the two lovebirds," Noah says.

I quickly slip out of Skye as my face turns redder—not because of embarrassment, but because my douche-bag friends were the ones who caused me to end that romp much sooner than I wanted to.

"I'm not talking to you until we are back home and in the office and I don't have a choice but to talk to you. Until then, leave me alone," I say as I turn my attention back to Skye, who is still pinned beneath me.

I know I wanted to fuck her every hour on the hour, but I'm not sure I can wait a whole hour to have her again. She's far too addictive for me to wait.

Noah laughs. The other two look at us with an amused grin on their faces, arms folded across their chests.

"You know they have bedrooms in this place for you to fuck in," Noah says with a wink.

I glare at him. I'm going to fire him when we get back home.

Skye laughs and pushes me off of her. I sit on the edge of the lounger while she turns and hangs her legs off, facing the men who are still standing, looking at us like they just found gold. But, if they think they are going to hang this over my head for the rest of eternity when we get back, they are wrong. They forget I'm their controlling boss who will fire them all if it comes to it.

"Actually, you were just who I was looking for," Skye says.

My glare turns from them to her. "What are you talking about?"

I know that Skye wants some kinky sex to make her forget about whatever she came here to forget, but if she's going to suggest a threesome with any one of these guys, I'm going to throw her over my shoulder and trap her in my room for the rest of the week. I won't share her. Not even with my best friends.

She ignores me, looking at them.

Noah sits down on the other lounger, curiously looking at her. "How can I be of help?"

"Well, this was supposed to be a *no-strings attached, hot romance* kind of thing for one week. But, unfortunately, a cat needed some rescuing the other day. The cat is fine now, but I had to show off some of my fabulous veterinarian skills, revealing far more about myself to Mr. Romantic here than I wanted. Now, he won't share anything with me to even the score. Care to share and get me caught up on him?"

"Noah is not saying anything," I say, looking at him dead in the eye, threatening more than his job if he says anything to her.

He smirks. "What do you want to know?" he asks, leaning closer to Skye.

"Something juicy. Because Mr. Romantic over here is acting far too perfect, and I know he has a darker side that he isn't showing me yet."

He glances at me while I continue to frown.

"He's being too romantic, huh?"

She nods.

"Hmm, that's shocking. I didn't think he had a romantic drop in his body."

"What do you mean?"

"I mean, he's a ruthless, controlling boss to us. A man who doesn't date. He doesn't do romance. All he cares about is money and pussy. Back home, he has a woman for every day of the week. So, whatever romantic he's pretending to be here, he's the exact opposite. It's a lie. He's nothing but a prick who will rip your heart out if you let him get too close."

I'm going to kill him. Here. Now. I won't even let him go back home. He's dead to me.

Skye smiles, placing her hand on his folded hands. "Thank you. That's just what I needed to hear."

I look at Skye like I'm looking at her for the first time. I thought she just wanted me to act cold toward her to help her keep from getting attached to me. That way, she couldn't have feelings toward me, and we could easily go our separate ways after this week. But I'm beginning to think it's more than that. She doesn't just want me to act distant toward her; she wants me to be cruel toward her. I'm missing something. A piece of her puzzle that I may never understand.

## 5

# SKYE

HE'S A BAD BOY, just like I wanted him to be. Every drop of romance he's given me has all been an act, most likely because he thought that was what he needed to do to get me into his bed. But, hopefully, now, he understands it's the exact opposite of what I want. I don't want a man who does anything more than kinky sex.

But still, from the look on Brody's face, he isn't too happy with his friends for revealing his true self to me. He doesn't realize that it's a blessing, not a curse, to know the truth. But he will.

"Skye, go to your room. I'll meet you there in five minutes," Brody commands.

I feel the familiar knots form deep in my belly at the thought of what he wants to do with me in my bedroom. We just had sex, but I'm nowhere near satiated, and it seems he isn't either.

I glance at his friends, silently wishing them luck, before I give in to Brody's command and head to my suite. I have a feeling that he's about to chew his friends out the second I leave, but I don't care as long as he keeps his promise and is knocking on my door within five minutes. If he doesn't keep his promise, I might have to punish him for not keeping his word.

I wait in my room for what seems like far longer than five minutes before I finally hear the rattle of his fist on the door. It's not a patient knock. Instead, it's an *if you don't open the door in three seconds, I'm going to knock the door down* kind of knock. So, as much as I want to swing the door open and jump into his waiting arms, I also want to make him even more pissed off than I'm sure he already is. The angrier he is, the better the sex is going to be. And I want the true bad boy he's been hiding from me to come out and play.

I make my feet drag on the tiled floor as I walk to the door in nothing but my bikini. I get to the wooden door separating us and take a deep breath as I hear him pound his fist on the door again. He's pissed. It's exuding off his body through the door to me. I bite my bottom lip as my lips curl up into a smile. I flip my wavy blue hair out of my face, and then I open the door with an amused smirk on my face as I look at Brody standing there with both hands grasping the doorframe. His face is dark, his nostrils are flared, and his eyes are full of rage. He looks like he doesn't know whether he's going to rip the door off the frame or punish me for taking so long to open the door. But I already know the answer. He's going to punish me. Hard. And I can't wait.

"Would you like to come in?" I ask smugly.

He drops his hands and walks into my suite, looking around at it like he wants to destroy every sparkling glass, every bottle of wine, every fancy lamp, and every piece of furniture in the room.

"Something wrong with my room?" I ask as I follow him into the bar area, which is large enough to function as a kitchen despite not having an actual stove or oven because there is no way anyone would actually cook on a vacation here.

He takes out a bottle of tequila and pours himself a drink

before he turns and glares at me as he rests his back against the counter.

"Nothing's wrong with your room. I have to remember that you didn't pay for it."

"Excuse me? I didn't pay for it?"

He gulps down the entire glass of tequila. Then, he grabs the bottle and pours some more into the glass. "Nope, you didn't. Your rich friend did."

I asked for a bad boy. I asked him to show me no emotions. I just didn't expect he'd turn into such an ass in a matter of seconds.

"First, I did pay for this suite. So, if your ego can't handle dating a woman who can afford a much nicer suite than you, you can leave."

I've never been so angry with a man in my life. He doesn't get to be pissed at me for having money that I earned.

"My ego can handle you making more money than me. I just don't believe that you do."

I frown. Hating him. That's all it took—one comment to make me go from begging for his body every second of every day to hating him.

"Second, you weren't supposed to Google me. We weren't supposed to know anything about each other."

He snorts. "Yeah, just like you weren't supposed to ask my friends anything about me."

"I asked one question about you because you already found out a fact about me. I was just returning the favor, but now that I know you were Googling me behind my back, I should have asked a lot more questions. Like why you are such a complete dick."

His lip twitches at that comment before he drinks down the rest of the tequila.

"Get out!" I say, not able to stand another second of his arrogant, chauvinistic ass.

"No." He pours himself another drink.

"You don't get to tell me no. I said, get the fuck out!"

He walks over to where I'm standing in the center of the kitchen, shaking from my anger. He holds the glass out to me, but I knock it onto the floor. The glass shatters as it hits the tiled floor. I don't care about the glass though. I care about getting this prick out of my life.

"I'll leave—after you admit what you really want, sweetheart."

He takes a step closer, and I take a step back until my back hits the counter behind me. He grins like the bastard he is as he traps me with his arms on either side of me, his body pushing up against me.

"I want you to leave," I say slowly, trying to squash the sparks flying around my body and lighting it up with a fire that only he has been able to start, and I have no idea how to put out the flames. I just want him gone. Then, I can get myself off in my Jacuzzi.

"No. What do you want? You said you wanted a bad boy. You wanted a man who didn't care about you. A man who takes what he wants from you with no regard for your feelings. You said you wanted a man to make you feel alive again and to make you forget about whatever you came here to forget. But, now that I am that man, you want me to leave. What. Do. You. Want?"

I can't breathe. I can't fucking breathe. His eyes are bearing down on me along with his entire body. Trapping me and consuming me. My body has never wanted him more than I do right now, and I hate myself for what I'm going to say next.

"You're right."

He cocks his head to one side with an amused expression on his face.

"What did you just say?" he asks even though he heard me clearly the first time.

"You. Are. Right. I wanted a bad boy, a man who didn't take care of me. A man who would play out all of my naughty fantasies in bed. Nothing more."

He nods. "And what do you want now?"

My eyes travel down his body. Over his hard chest and rippling abs that I want to trace my tongue over until I've felt every hard ridge. Down to his swim trunks that barely contain his erection as it pushes in my bare stomach. I want his body. I want his indifference to me. I want him to treat me like shit, so when we go our separate ways, I will feel nothing toward him, except hatred and a longing to find another man who can fuck me like he did.

He can treat me like an ass, and I'll do the same right back. That's the only way this will work.

"I want you. I want you to fuck me. I want you to be your true self. An asshole. A prick. A man I will never think of again after this week, except for how his cock felt when he fucked me."

"Done, baby," he says as his lips claim mine.

The kiss is aggressive, carnal, full of threats about what he's going to do with my body. It's exactly what I want even if it feels a bit dangerous at the same time.

I kiss back, throwing everything I can into the kiss. My tongue pushes into his mouth, dancing with his, letting him know that I might want him to take control, but I won't give up that control easily. I nip at his lip, nibbling hard.

He growls and grabs my face, forcing me to stop.

"I don't know what happened to you to make you hate men so much, but you're about to hate and love me so much that whatever happened in your past is nothing more than a blip on your radar."

I suck in a breath at his admission. He can Google me all he wants, but he'll never learn enough about my past to really know me. He can guess all he wants about what man broke my heart in the past and how, but he'll never know the truth.

He smirks. "You want dirty?" he whispers into my ear.

"Yes," I exhale as he kisses my ear.

"You want to be tied up and in pain?"

"Yes."

"You want me to tell you what I whispered in your ear during the competition?"

"Yes."

He turns his head and glances at the clock that says two minutes till one o'clock. He turns back around with a sly grin on his face.

"I said that I was going to tie you up and fuck you every hour on the hour for twenty-four hours straight. That you wouldn't be able to sleep or eat or sit straight because all you could think about while the minutes passed between fuckings was my cock. How desperate you were for it. How you ached between your legs for me to fuck you. How your lips begged to be wrapped around my long, thick length. How your body trembled, waiting for me."

My mouth drops as I think about it. I've never fucked a man more than twice in a day. I can't imagine twenty-four times. I don't think he can do it. That's impossible. But I watch the clock as the seconds tick by behind him, inching closer to the next hour. We started at noon. That leaves twenty-three more times. That's far too many and somehow also not enough. I'm not sure if a week is long enough to get Brody out of my system. But I need to try.

I watch as the clock changes to one o'clock, and Brody's face comes alive with a darkness I haven't seen from him before.

He spins me around before I realize what's happening. My arms are forced together behind my back, and then I feel something slick going around my wrists as he forcefully ties them together.

"A tie?" I ask, confused about where he got it.

"Yes. I grabbed the damn thing from my room before I came here. It's the one that Bayron pressured me into wearing last night. I've finally found a way to put it to good use."

He tightens it, roughly tying it around my wrists, so tightly that there is no way I will ever be able to break free. He grabs my arm and leads me out toward the balcony that overlooks my private pool. He pushes me down until I'm kneeling in front of him before he pulls out his thick, erect cock.

"Suck," he commands.

I want to, but I don't want to at the same time. I want to feel his cock filling my mouth. I want to suck the pleasure out of him, but I don't want to give him any pleasure at the same time because he's a dick.

"Suck," he says again as he pushes his cock at my lips.

My eyes light up in defiance, as I open my mouth to let his cock in, but I don't plan on letting him get the pleasure that he is seeking. I barely let my lips cover his tip as I suck him, licking the pre-cum off that has settled over the tip.

He grabs my hair in his fist, and I know he is going to force my head further over his cock but not until I rake my teeth over his length hard enough that I know it isn't entirely pleasant.

"Cunt," he curses with a wicked grin on his face.

He likes it when I defy him. He wants me to. Just like I want him to punish me for defying him.

And then he pushes his dick so far into my throat that I can't help but gag.

"Breathe, gorgeous," he says before he pulls his cock back out of my mouth before slowly pushing it back in again.

This time, I'm prepared. I breathe calmly as the tears stain down my face from the pain, but the look on his face makes it all worth it.

The groans leaving his throat make me want to suck him in deeper. And the pain pushes all of my real pain away, just like I thought it would. I want more and more and more of this. More pain.

He sees it in my eyes when I surrender to the pain, and instead of fighting it, I crave more. His lip twitches, and his eyes come alive when he realizes that this is actually what I want. That I'm not going to say *red* when he pushes his cock down my throat, I'm not going to say it when he hits me too hard on the ass, I'm not going to say it when his cock is thrusting too hard inside. Instead, I'm going to beg for more.

He grabs my arm, forcing me back onto my feet. He kisses me, tasting himself on my lips. My body aches for him every time he kisses me. My pussy aches for him, desperate to have the same cock that was filling me earlier inside me.

"Trust me, Skye," he commands. It should be a question, but it isn't. I realize nothing with him will ever be a question again.

He grabs my thighs and lifts me up, spreading my legs open as he sits me on the railing. I squeal as he does it. Both from the sudden movement and from being thrust up onto a railing where I could fall over the edge and die.

I glance over my shoulder. We aren't that high up, not even a full story. I might not die if I fell, but I would definitely break something. The problem is, my hands are still tied behind my back. I can't hold on to anything. I'm entirely under his control. My life is literally in his hands.

"Brody, no—"

But then his tongue is licking my pussy as his hands spread me wider, and I forget that I could die. At least I'd die happy. He licks me, taking in every drop of liquid that pours out of my body. His tongue dances over my clit as I make sounds that I didn't even know my throat could make. I went from incredible pain to incredible pleasure in a second. From fear to ecstasy.

And I know that, in a second, he could flip a switch and bring me right back to the pain.

"God, don't ever stop," I groan so loudly that I'm sure all the rooms next to us can hear me.

"God, huh? Why does he get the credit for all my hard work?"

He flicks his tongue over my clit again.

"Brody," I cry out.

"That's better," he moans against my clit, causing me to shake from the electricity that he just shot through my body.

I feel my body falling backward. I tense my abs, holding myself up, an almost impossible task, even for someone as in shape as I am, while he's doing what he's doing to my body with his tongue.

"Brody, help," I cry.

He stops for a second. "You'd better hold yourself up because I'm a little busy here," he says with a wink.

"I hate you," I cry as he tortures me again with his tongue.

"I know, but you don't know what hate is yet."

I try to focus on keeping my balance instead of what he's doing to my body, which is almost impossible because he's far too good at what he's doing. I'm about to come, and I'm not sure how I can keep my balance and come at the same time.

*He won't let you fall*, the voice in my head reminds me. *He's just teasing you.*

I hope.

So, instead of focusing on staying upright, I focus on his tongue lapping over my clit. I focus on that feeling deep in my gut that keeps getting stronger.

"I'm going to..."

The second I start to come, he stops, and I come on nothing. His fingers disappear from my pussy, his tongue stops licking my clit, and my orgasm is far less exceptional than I expected. Because he fucking stopped.

His hands let go of me, and he licks my juices off of his fingers, one by one. I stare intently at him, not believing what he just did, as I forget that I'm the only one now holding me up onto the balcony.

I start falling. I try to engage my abs and my legs to keep myself from falling, but I'm not sure if I'm strong enough to hold myself up. Not anymore.

My body slips off backward, and I know my last chance is if I can hook my leg under the railing to keep me from falling to the ground below me. My leg catches at the same time that Brody's hands grab on to my waist.

Together, we pull me back up.

"You almost let me die!" I pant and scream.

He puts his fingers over my lips, shushing me. "No, I pushed you to your limit to teach you how to live."

I breathe hard and fast, wanting to yell at him more, but he's right. Deep down, I loved that. I loved the thrill that anything could happen. The only part I didn't love was not getting to experience my full orgasm because of him.

"What's wrong, princess?" he asks with a smirk.

"You didn't let me come."

"I know. But you will now."

He grabs me, shoving me face-first toward the railing with my ass in the air. His hands grab my hips, and I feel his cock pushing at my ass. He's going to fuck me in the ass. I know it. I bite my lip to keep from begging him not to. I've never been fucked in the ass before, and as scary as it sounds, I want to feel it. I want to know how dirty and painful sex can be. I want to feel all of it. It's the only way I can move on with my life.

His cock pushes at my ass as it taunts me but doesn't actually enter me.

"You want me to fuck your ass, don't you, Skye?" he asks, his voice sultry and full of promises that I'm not sure I'm ready for.

"Yes," I groan, keeping my eyes closed rather than looking down at how far I could have fallen.

"Oh, I will but not yet. You aren't ready. Your pussy, on the other hand"—his fingers dip inside me, two, three, four, stretching me wider than I've ever been stretched—"is very ready." He pulls his fingers back out and immediately replaces them with his cock pushing hard into me.

"Jesus," I growl as I'm pushed hard into the railing as he fucks me from behind, sliding in and out of me like he's been fucking me his whole life and knows exactly what my body craves.

He thrusts, and I know that, after not coming hard enough earlier, it won't take me long to come. And I plan on coming hard on his cock. I won't let him take my pleasure from me again.

"You almost there?" he asks, not needing to ask the question because he already knows the answer.

I pant hard because I can't form any words or process what he's saying. I can't concentrate on anything but the wave consuming me. An explosion of feelings as my orgasm starts deep in my belly and then takes over every fiber in my body.

I feel his palm on my ass as he hits me hard at the peak of my orgasm. I've never experienced pain like that during sex. I thought it was meant as a punishment, but when his palm touches my body, I finally understand what the pain is really meant to bring. A pleasure I've never felt before and a connection to the man who gives me that feeling. I let a man tie me up, hold my life in his hands, and slap my ass hard. It's not something I would trust every man with. But, after this, I would trust Brody with any part of my body. I trust him with bringing me the best sex I've ever felt or ever thought I could feel.

He pulls out of me, and I feel my body falling to the floor in complete exhaustion. I love running and working out. But I have nothing left in me. I've never felt so exhausted after sex.

I feel his arms scooping me up and lifting me off the ground. My head falls against his chest as I close my eyes. I could easily sleep in his arms just like this if he held me. He carries me back inside and gently lays me on the bed. I wait for him to go around to my arms to untie me and then climb into bed with me. I'm sure he is just as exhausted as I am.

He leans down, and I feel his lips against my ear. "Sleep tight, baby. You have thirty-five minutes until you'll be coming with my cock deep inside your gorgeous pussy." He nips at my ear and then stands back up.

I glance at the clock. Thirty-five minutes. It's not nearly enough time to rest if every time is going to be like that. But, somehow, my pussy is already aching for another fuck with him. I've turned into a greedy monster that can't get enough of his body.

I watch him walk away from the slits that my eyes have become. I can't even bring myself to open them all the way.

"Where are you going?" I whisper. Even my voice is not working properly.

He smirks as he stops, standing naked at the foot of the bed, before he grabs his trunks and pulls them back on.

"To get some new toys to torture you with to play with in thirty-three minutes," he says, somehow always knowing exactly how much time remains without ever looking at the clock.

I swallow hard, thinking about what he could be bringing back. A whip, crop, rope, butt plug, what? I doubt that he thought to bring all those things with him when he didn't know that he was going to find a woman who craved those things, but maybe he did. Or maybe he's going to find a creative solution to finding new toys to play with. Whatever he does, I don't care. I want him. The toys are just a bonus.

He's the most exciting thing I've ever felt. I've never been so consumed with the need for sex, but now, I don't know how I've lived without sex that takes over everything.

He starts walking toward the door.

"Are you going to untie me?"

He stops and turns his head to look at me, deadpan. "No."

And then he turns and walks out the door, leaving my arms tied behind my back, as I lie in the bed, naked except for my own cum still dripping down between my legs. Damn this man. Even when he's gone, he makes sure that all I can do is think about him. I close my eyes while I try to decide if choosing Brody over all the other men was the best or worst thing I've ever done in my life. It's too soon to decide. But I do know one thing. Brody has just ruined sex for me with all other men.

6

———

**BRODY**

THIS WOMAN.

I can't get her out of my head. She owns me. My thoughts. My body. My cock. Everything. It's hers.

I've only known her a week, but in that week, I've fucked her in almost every way my dirty brain can come up with. I've tied her up in ways I thought no woman could actually bend. I've pushed her limits, fucking her in public places, over balconies, in restaurants. I've made her bleed, caused bruises, and heard her cry out from the pain of my hand or a whip on her ass or thigh. None of it was enough.

It wasn't enough for me.

And it sure wasn't enough for her.

I know everything there is to know about her body. I know the whimpers she makes when she is begging me for more. I know just how far her body can last before she's lost to her orgasm. I know exactly what buttons to push on her body to make her come seconds after our first kiss. I know how hard to hit her ass to make her cheeks just the right shade of pink.

I know all of that, yet the only personal thing I know about her is that she's a veterinarian who has a rich friend, who's a princess, and that she came here to forget something. I know that I'm the first man she's been with who she's had dark, dangerous sex with and that, most likely, after today, when she goes back home, she'll go back to her normal ways. She will date normal men who take her on normal dates and have normal sex.

She won't beg them to tie her up. She won't ache for them to control her body with whips and chains. She'll pretend she is a nice, sweet girl that wants a nice, caring man. She'll search for a man to marry, to raise kids with. She'll forget about her dark urges and me.

I'm not sure if I can handle that. I won't let her forget about me. I need one more fuck that will make it impossible for her to forget me. Something that will push her limits further than I've ever pushed her. Which is going to be hard since I fucked her on the hour for twenty-four hours straight and then at least three times a day the rest of the week. Each time I fucked her, I tried to come up with something that would make her use her safe word to make me stop.

She never did. Not even close.

Skye rolls over in bed with a grin on her face. Even though her eyes are still closed, she knows that I'm in bed with her. It's a strange feeling at first—to wake up in a bed with a woman, but how quickly that faded after the first night we spent together. Now, I can't imagine not waking up to her sweet face and getting a good fuck in before we even leave the bed.

"What are you thinking?" she asks, able to read my body and mind without even opening her eyes.

It's freaky how well we know each other's bodies.

"About how I want to fuck you on our last day together."

Her eyes flicker open as she licks her bottom lip. "What do you have in mind?"

I can't help but smile at her reaction. I've never been with a woman who wanted sex as much as I do, but Skye is definitely that woman. She's never satiated. I think I could spend every second of every day trying to make that happen, and it never would.

I stroke her face, trying to memorize every feature of her face to take with me.

"What is something you've always wanted to do on vacation?" I ask.

"You," she says, giggling a little.

I shake my head. "Other than sex, my dirty girl. What's something you've always wanted to do but never did? Or have you done it all? The snorkeling, the swimming with dolphins, the zip-lining."

She thinks for a second.

"You've done all of that, haven't you?" I ask.

She winces. "Yeah, as much as I've probably convinced you that all I do on vacations is fuck complete strangers for a week, it's not true. I usually spend my time going on adventures. It beats just sitting on the beach and drinking alone every day."

I frown. I can't imagine her ever being lonely, but it seems that, for at least part of her life, she has been.

I tuck her hair behind her ear as I gently and lazily kiss her on the lips, not wanting it to go any further than a kiss right now but needing to taste her to make her not feel alone at least for a second.

She smiles sweetly when I stop kissing her.

"Why do you want to know?"

I shrug. "Just trying to think of a way to spice up our last few fucks together."

She laughs. "I don't think that's possible, not after last night."

My eyes glaze over as I think about last night. I fucked her in the ass while she was tied up to one of the curtains backstage at one of the performances that the resort puts on. All the time, any of the performers had to do in order to see her was glance to their left, and they would have seen us fucking. Only one ever did at the very end, but I don't think she got a good look at what was happening.

"You're probably right. That was a great night. Almost as good as the fifth time I fucked you."

I watch her eyes glaze over with thoughts of that night. It doesn't take her long to get the fire in her eyes as she finally remembers that time. It was the first time I used a whip on her. I can still remember the excitement and shock that covered her face when I first touched the cold whip to her bare skin.

A rattling sound on the door tears us both from our reliving our highlights of the week.

"Room service?" I ask, raising an eyebrow as I climb out of bed.

Her eyes follow me, lingering over my dick as I pull my boxers on.

"Maybe," she finally says, thinking.

I shrug and walk to the door. I never order room service unless I plan on eating the food off her body. In fact, I haven't done a nice thing for her all week unless you count giving her too many orgasms. The only reason I'm even opening the door to her suite for her is to keep her in the bed, naked, as long as I can.

I open the door, expecting breakfast and instead find Bayron.

I frown and stand firmly in the doorway. I would slam the door in his face without saying a word, but I'm guessing he's here to tell Skye when people will arrive to pack her things and about her leaving instructions. I only allow him a moment to tell me that's what he's here for because ensuring that other people are taking care of her packing means I get more time with her today.

"I need to speak with Miss Skye," he says, ignoring me.

I fold my arms across my chest, standing more firmly in the

doorway. "You can tell me, and I'll make sure she gets the message."

He shakes his head like he expected me to say that and it's ridiculous. "Fine. Tell Miss Skye I have a message from Gabe. I'll be waiting here for her to tell me what she wants me to do about it."

I roll my eyes as I slam the door in his face and walk back to Skye. I don't know who Gabe is, but whoever he is, I'm sure that she won't give a fuck what he has to say, not when she has me to keep her fully occupied the rest of the day. Gabe can wait until tonight when she's back in the real world.

"Was that Bayron?" Skye asks, amused. She knows how I feel about Bayron.

"Yes," I say, falling back onto the bed next to her. I was going to wait to fuck her until I came up with some crazy way to fuck her. While parasailing or something, but my dick needs her pussy now. I don't even feel like tying her up or spanking her. I just need a good, fast, hard fuck.

I grab her and pull her on top of my body until she is straddling me, my dick growing hard underneath her pussy that will quickly drench me as her hips thrust over me. I grab her hair that is tangled from sleep and pull her face to mine so that I can kiss her luscious lips. She easily gives in, always prepared for sex because she wants it as badly as I do.

She moans into my lips as I push my tongue hard into her mouth, dancing with her tongue as I press our bodies tighter together. I watch her eyes roll back in her head as my cock pushes against her tight cunt.

"What do you want, baby?" I ask. I never ask what she wants. There's no need. I know. Her body gives me more than enough clues of what she wants.

"I want—"

Rattling on the door stops Skye in her tracks as she looks at me again, amused at what Bayron could have possibly said to me that would make me come back and fuck her to distract her and me.

"What did Bayron want?" she asks.

I shake my head. "Nothing. Here's your last chance to get anything you want from me. You want it slow and easy. You want to take control. You want to tie me up. I'll do anything you want. A one-time chance. What do you want?"

Her grin widens as she leans down and kisses me hard and firm on the lips but doesn't push her tongue into my mouth like I want her to.

"You're being bad, trying to distract me, because you don't want me to do whatever nonsense Bayron wants me to do, but if I miss my flight because of you, you're going to be in big trouble, mister. So, tell me what Bayron wanted, and then you can get back to fucking me however you want."

I glare at her, trying to convince her with my eyes that she doesn't want to know what Bayron said, but it only makes her more adorable. She won't give in to my glares or charm.

I sigh. "Something about you having a phone call from someone. It was nothing. He said he'd wait out in the hallway for a few minutes until you decided what you wanted to do about it. I wouldn't worry about it. You're going to be home in twelve hours, and you can call them back then."

She nods and leans down, her lips hovering over mine to kiss me again when she stops.

"Who?" she asks suddenly.

I shrug. "Gabe."

"Oh," she says, her body freezing as her eyes grow wide.

I raise an eyebrow at her reaction, but I don't ask the obvious question. *Who is Gabe?* I want to know. *Is he her brother? Father? Child? Her dog? Best friend? Or Lover?*

I'd be fine with most of those answers. I don't care if she has a kid. But I don't want to know about a current or ex-lover. She's still mine for the next eight hours until she has to leave for the airport.

She rolls off me and onto her back before she bounces off the edge of the bed and begins putting her clothes back on.

"What are you doing?"

She ignores me and continues to put clothes on.

I jump out of the bed, still only wearing my boxers and now a hard-on that won't go away anytime soon.

"Skye?" I ask, standing in front of her, not letting her go talk to Bayron until she talks to me first.

She shakes her head, snapping out of whatever spell she has been under the last few seconds that made her forget that I was even here.

"Sorry. I should go speak to Bayron. Just give me five minutes, and then we can get back to what we do best," she says, smiling. She quickly kisses me on the lips and then slips under my arm and out to the door.

I don't know what just happened, but I don't have a good feeling about it. She smiled at me, but it wasn't genuine. She kissed me, but she kissed me like she was kissing a brother. With nothing behind it.

I consider chasing after her and dragging her back inside to demand she tell me what the hell is going on, but I don't. That's not what we are. We are fuck buddies. I don't get to ask about her life, and she doesn't get to ask about my life.

I consider jacking off while I wait. It will give me something to keep me distracted, but I'd rather jack off in her. So, I wait. I walk to the kitchenette and pull out leftovers from our meal last night. I start eating them to stop my mind from thinking too hard. I quickly eat the fried chicken, annoyed that she isn't back. I start pacing, walking all the way to the front door to try to listen to her conversation with Bayron before I walk back to the bedroom. Whatever she is talking to Bayron about, she isn't angry or upset or frustrated. She seems calm, happy even. That only makes my own frustration grow.

Finally, the door swings open, and a bouncing Skye walks back into the bedroom, but her grin quickly disappears the second she sees me frowning at her.

"Did your conversation go well?" I ask.

"Yes," she says, swallowing hard.

"And?" I ask, waiting for her to elaborate.

She bites her lip, and I know whatever it is, it's very bad for me. She only ever bites her lip when she's nervous or she wants to be fucked. And, right now, I think it's a little of both.

"I have to leave...now."

My mouth drops open at that. Of all the things I imagined her saying when she returned, that wasn't one of them.

"Why?"

"Does it matter?"

I narrow my eyes, walking toward her. "Yes, it fucking matters when it takes away time I was supposed to have with you."

Her eyes look away from me, toward her closet full of clothes that I'm sure she's thinking about needing to get packed.

I grab her chin and turn her face to mine so that I can see her. "Why. Are. You. Leaving?"

"I'm sorry," she says, narrowing her eyes at me as she pulls herself out of my grasp. She walks to the closet and pulls out a suitcase. She opens it, laying it on the bed before she returns to the closet and begins pulling out heaps of clothes and then placing them into the suitcase.

"What are you doing?"

"Packing." She continues to throw clothes into the suitcase, not even bothering to fold them.

I move in front of the suitcase as she holds another large pile of clothes in her hands.

"Stop."

"I have to pack," she says, trying to move around me to put the clothes into the suitcase.

I block her. "Stop. The staff can pack for you. You need to talk to me."

She shakes her head. "There is nothing to say."

I frown. This is not how we are going to end. She doesn't get to stop this by just ignoring me and then leaving. That's not how our story ends. Our story ends with great sex and with a twinkle at the thought that, someday, we could run into each other and have great sex again. But that we didn't let our personal lives affect us. That we meant something to each other because what we had was perfect and untouched by the real world.

I pick her up and carry her to the other side of the bed that isn't currently holding a suitcase. I throw her down and pin her to the bed with my body as I lean down and kiss her.

She doesn't kiss me back. She doesn't fight me off either. She does nothing. It's like she isn't even really here. She just stares off into space.

I search her eyes for some clue as to what is going on. I find nothing.

"Who is Gabe?" I ask because I'm desperate. And, even if Gabe is a boyfriend, I need to hear it. I need to know that he is the reason she's rushing home. I need to be angry with someone and not direct it all at her. I don't want to hate her. I need to know why she is thinking about another man instead of me.

She swallows, and finally, I see a little of the fire in her eyes that I'm used to seeing.

"A man who needs me."

I smirk and rub my dick against her thigh. "Right now, no man can need you more than I do."

I expect a smile. A laugh, even. I get neither, just a sad woman with sad eyes.

"If he makes you this sad, why go back to him?"

She swallows. "Because, despite what you know about me, I'm not this person. I don't fuck random men. I don't push people away and forget all of my troubles. That's not who I am. I care deeply about everyone around me. I take care of them even if they don't deserve it. I take care of them even if it hurts me."

I hate him. Whatever he's done to her to make her like this makes me want to hunt him down to the ends of the earth. I want to make him pay for hurting her. I want her to stop feeling like she has to take care of him.

"Stop looking at me like that," she says, her voice soft from beneath me.

"I can't."

She shakes her head. "We don't do this. We don't share personal things with each other. We don't have feelings for each other. We have sex. And it was great while it lasted. You were the distraction I desperately needed this week. You let me be selfish. You let me forget. But, now, our time is up. It's time to return to the real world where we face real problems."

"I need one more fuck."

She closes her eyes rather than looking at me. "We don't get to fuck anymore."

I kiss her again, desperate to get the one more time that we are both owed. She still won't kiss me back. She's already closing herself off to me, and she hasn't even left yet.

"Kiss me, Skye. Let me fuck you. Let me make you forget. One more time."

"No," she says as her eyes open, and she gently pushes me off her body. She swings her legs over the edge of the bed, sitting up. "I need to leave in ten minutes for the airport."

She starts walking to the door, and I follow her. She opens it, standing behind the door, and I know what she is going to ask me to do.

"Good-bye, Brody."

She doesn't kiss me or hug me. She barely even looks at me. I don't have a chance right now to change her mind. I'm not asking for forever, just one more time. But, apparently, that isn't going to happen. We are done.

I pull on some clothes and step out of her suite like she wants because, short of actually kidnapping her or tying her up for real, I don't have any choices left. I hear the door shut behind me, and I feel a stabbing in my body that I wasn't expecting whenever we said good-bye. But maybe it is because this isn't how we were supposed to say good-bye.

I turn and see Bayron standing in the hallway, looking at me with sadness in his eyes as well. I can't stand any more gloom today. And I definitely can't deal with him lecturing me right now about how I broke Skye's heart. If her heart is broken, she did it to herself.

"Would you pass a message along to Skye?" I ask Bayron.

He smiles tightly. "Yes."

7

———

**SKYE**

I LEAN my back against the door to remain standing instead of falling to the floor in a puddle like I really want to do. I did the right thing. It was time to say good-bye. My normal life is calling, and Brody does not fit into my normal life. But it still hurts.

Not because I love him. I don't.

Not because I care for him. I do, but I care for a lot of people. It's not what's making me hurt.

Not because I ever imagined any sort of future with Brody. I didn't.

It hurts because this wasn't how we were supposed to end. We were supposed to go out with a bang. Literally. Not with an unexpected good-bye, as I'm being pulled back into a life I don't know how to escape from.

A knock on the door gets my heart racing with far too much hope. I know Brody is standing on the other side of the door, and he's going to try to convince me one last time to fuck him. And I don't have the strength to say no again. Despite not having the time, I don't care. I need to forget. One more time.

I turn around and throw the door open with a smile on my face.

"Bayron," I say, my lips and heart instantly falling.

"He's gone, Miss Skye," Bayron says, reading my thoughts.

"Oh."

"Are you ready for my staff to get you packed up?"

I nod.

He motions to the staff behind him to enter. I step aside to let them pass. I know they will have me packed up in a matter of minutes, and then I'll have nothing left to do but leave.

"He wanted me to give you a message," he says.

I bite my lip, trying to calm down. It's probably just a good-bye. He never gave me a good-bye.

"Do you want to hear it?"

I nod.

"He said that this isn't good-bye. That you aren't finished. He gets one more day. One more time. That was what the agreement was. Seven days. You've fulfilled only six of those days. He said he'll be waiting for you at the airport."

He's going to meet me at the airport. I know it. The grin and life in my cheeks returns.

"Thank you, Bayron. For everything." I lean forward and kiss him on the cheek.

"Be careful, Miss Skye," he says.

"I will," I say, knowing that he means be careful about Brody even though he isn't the one I should be worried about. I put up a barrier between us the second I met him. Brody isn't the problem. Gabe is.

The fact that I'm ending my last day early to run back to Gabe only verifies that he's the problem I don't know how to move on from. He's the one who broke my heart. I never gave Brody the same chance. It's impossible for him to break my heart when I never gave it to him in the first place.

———

I arrive at the airport with excitement and anxiety. My legs haven't been able to stop shaking since I got into the car. I've tried to enjoy the last few minutes of my time in paradise by looking at the beautiful scenery as I am driven to the airport, but nothing holds my attention.

I glance at the clock on the driver's dashboard as he pulls up in front of the airport. I have thirty minutes until my flight. More than enough time to fuck Brody one last time in a restroom before going through security and still making my flight.

I step out of the car and talk to the ticket agent to get my bags checked before I start looking for him.

He's here somewhere; I know it. I pull my phone out of my purse, looking at it before I realize that I don't even have his phone number. I don't even know his last name. I know nothing about him that would allow me to find him.

I could talk to Bayron. He'd give me whatever information he had on Brody if I wanted him to, but I don't. I don't want to know personal details. I just want his body one last time.

I scan the airport lobby, but I don't immediately see him. I know that I can't walk through security. He'll have no chance at finding me there. His flight back home isn't until much later in the day. So, I walk over and take a seat on a bench, and I wait, letting in thoughts of Brody and igniting my deepest desires to have him one last time.

---

*My eyes widen when I see him pull the rope out from behind his back. In the last few days with him, I've learned that I love being tied up. I love giving him control over my body. He knows his way around my body better than I do. But even though I've started to trust him these last couple of days, my heart still beats faster and the adrenaline shoots through me whenever he does something even a little bit dangerous.*

*"Hand," he says. One word, but he commands my soul with it.*

*I hold out my left hand and he begins tying the rope around my wrist. He looks to my other hand and I hold it out for him as well. He ties my hands together making sure that the rope is tight enough that I can't escape, but not so tight that it will leave a mark.*

*And then he pulls my arms above my head as he ties my wrists to the headboard. My arms instinctually pull at the rope testing to see if I can escape or not. I can't.*

*I don't understand why I give him so much control. I don't understand why I trust him, especially given my past with men, but I do.*

*He pulls out another rope and I pant.*

*He's only ever tied my hands up, so it thrills and terrifies me to find out what it will feel like to completely give up everything to him.*

*He grabs my ankle and takes his time tying a rope around each leg. Then stretches my legs wide as he attaches them to each of the posts on the foot of the bed.*

*"Do you trust me?"*

*"Yes," I breathe.*

*"Good."*

*He tosses his shirt over my face, covering my eyes. I wait for him to tie it around my head, but he never does. I can't see him, but it wouldn't take much for me to shake the shirt off my face if I wanted to.*

*I don't though.*

*His hands go to my bikini top and he pushes it up off my breasts. Then his fingers hook into the sides of my bikini bottoms, and he slowly pulls them down until I'm naked, completely at his disposal.*

*I wait for him to kiss me. Stroke me. Spank me. Anything.*

*He doesn't.*

*He waits. He's far too patient.*

*Every second that passes I grow more restless trying to anticipate what he's going to do. He's left me alone before; is that what he's doing again? Leaving me to suffer while he goes and finds new toys?*

He hasn't left though. I can't see him, but I can feel him. He's here. I can barely hear him breathing. It's calm and steady, unlike my own that races faster with every second that passes.

"Please," I whisper, needing him so badly that I can't stand it. I pull at the ropes, needing to get my hands on him, but I can't. And he doesn't offer me any relief.

More times passes. It feels like hours to me, even though I know in reality it's only been a few minutes.

Cold. I feel ice cold hit my nipple and I gasp from the unexpected touch. My back arches and my body writhes underneath his mouth.

I feel him use his mouth to move the ice over my other nipple. He swirls it around while my body moves beneath his.

He moves it down my stomach until he lets his slide off over my pussy.

Goosebumps shoot over my body, as I shiver from both the cold and the need for his body.

Again he makes me wait, but much shorter this time before I feel hot drip over my nipples.

"Fuck," I gasp, as the hot mixes with the cold sensation and takes over my body.

I don't know what he's dripping over my body, but it's a feeling I've never felt before. It makes my entire body come alive.

"God damn, I love your body," he says.

I bite my lip as I arch my back again. "I need you."

I can feel him smirk. "Not until you can't stand not to have my dick inside you a second longer, only then."

I struggle against the ropes again. "I can't wait."

His lips touch my neck and I groan.

"Not yet."

His fingers trail down my body far too slowly before he curls his fingers around my pussy and pushes two inside.

*"Yes," I moan.*

*"So wet baby."*

*He slowly pulls his finger in and out of my pussy and my juices cover his fingers, begging for him.*

*"I'm ready."*

*"Not yet," he says again.*

*He pulls his fingers out and then his tongue replaces his fingers at my entrance. He pushes it inside me before pulling it back out and licking over my clit.*

*I've never felt anything so intense. I've never needed sex more.*

*"I'm going to come," I scream, as he licks me again.*

*"Come."*

*He moves his tongue faster over me and I can't contain my orgasm. I come over his tongue and lips.*

*I feel his grin against me, as my body trembles from the intensity of my orgasm.*

*I'm spent.*

*I'm exhausted from waiting, and then going through all the emotions I felt before finally coming. I still want his cock, but I'm not sure I can take much more.*

*"Fuck me," I plead.*

*He grins. "Not until you come again."*

*"I can't."*

*But his tongue darts inside me again and I feel my body give into him, despite my brain saying that I can't take much more. His hands grab my thighs pushing me open, as my body pulls against the ropes holding me down.*

*It doesn't take me long before I'm coming over his tongue again.*

*"You taste so good."*

*"I need your co—"*

*He doesn't let me finish my sentence. He makes me come again and again. And only when he knows that my body can't take any more, does he finally drive his cock inside me. It's never felt so good to have his cock inside me as it does right now. I've never needed sex as much as I do right now.*

———

My body aches to have Brody one last time. My eyes dart around the airport, but I don't see him. He's making me wait again. I'm fine waiting, but I'm already so turned on that I could come with one kiss from him. I try to think about something else while I wait. And wait. And wait. My thoughts keep going back to Brody though.

I wait until I barely have enough time to go through security, pee, and make my flight. And then I go. I walk through security and then onto my flight. I try not to think of him as I board. I have more important things to focus my attention on and worry about now. But Brody is all I can think about as the cabin door closes and the engines purr to life.

I feel hurt, empty, broken. I feel things I never thought Brody could make me feel. *Why didn't he show up?* That's all I can think about as we push back from the gate. Maybe something happened to him. He was hurt. His car got into an accident. It doesn't make me feel especially better, but it does make me think that he's not that big of an ass. That he did want to fuck me, but he just couldn't get to me for whatever reason.

My phone buzzes in my hands. I haven't switched it to Airplane Mode yet, like I'm supposed to. It's a message from an unknown number.

I bite my lip as I stare at my phone. I know it's Brody. I just don't know if I should open it or not. I hear the engines roar louder, and I know we are about to take off soon and that I won't have a chance to look at the message again until we land.

I click the message to open it, praying that he didn't get into a car accident and is now dying in the hospital while I fly thousands of miles away.

He's not dying.

He's not hurt.

He's not even texting to apologize.

Instead, I get a picture of him with a blonde with fake boobs and a fake smile sitting on his lap on a lounge chair back at the resort. His arms are wrapped around her as he softly kisses her on the cheek.

I read the words that he typed below the picture.

*I got a little distracted and couldn't make it. Sorry I'm such a dick.*

I delete the image and his number from my phone before I have a chance to do something stupid like texting him back. I reach into my purse and pull out my headphones to put on and try to entertain myself with music or a movie. Even though I know neither will be enough to distract me from Brody.

I thought, the entire flight back, all I would be thinking about was Gabe and how to handle him. Instead, I feel a hatred I've never felt for a man before. And I've felt plenty of hatred for men before. Gabe did a number on me just before I came here.

Brody thinks he's a prick, and he is. That's what I wanted when I came here. An asshole who would make it easy for me to forget about him once I left here. I didn't realize just how much of an asshole he could be. And I made a mistake, thinking it would be easy for me to forget about a dick like Brody after I left. It will be easy to move on from him to another guy when I get back, but I won't be able to forget him. This hatred that I feel will stay with me for far too long after I return home. Brody won't be forgotten, just hated. And I have a feeling that is exactly what he wanted. He isn't the kind of man who would allow me to forget.

8

———

**BRODY**

I HEAR a knock on my office door for the hundredth time today. I exhale deeply to keep from doing what I want to do. Telling my assistant to call everyone in the building and demand they all go home so that I can get some real work done. I have a shit-ton of papers to go through and more emails to answer than I could possibly read, and I have some important decisions to make in regard to if we are going to be ready for the launch of our video game that happens in less than three weeks. Because, if we aren't ready, I need to save the company millions of dollars and postpone it now rather than waiting.

"Come in," I snarl at whoever is behind the oak door.

I like my office closed off from the world. The door is solid, the same with the walls. No one can see into my world unless I let them. I don't even have that many windows to look outside. I might be the most important person at the company, but I don't have the nicest office, just the most secluded. But it doesn't prevent me from having to deal with idiots knocking on my door all day.

The door opens, and a young woman steps inside. She's probably in her early twenties. She looks put together but far too eager to be in my office right now. She hasn't been yelled at nearly enough to have the look of despair that everyone else in my office knows well enough to wear on their faces when they enter my office. I'm a controlling fucker who wants things done my way. The proper way. I don't accept mistakes. You get one shot to impress me, and if you don't, you're gone.

The woman standing in front of me is already failing. She thinks she's going to impress me because she looks good in her light-colored skirt and jacket. She's wrong. It takes a lot more than lean legs to get me off.

"Did you forget why you came in here?" I ask, glaring at her for interrupting me and wasting my valuable time. I make far too much money for this company to waste a single second of it not on point.

She smiles, clearly not getting the message I'm sending. "I'm Angela," she says, walking toward me with her hand extended to me.

I look down at her hand, not bothering to shake it.

"What are you doing in my office, Angela?"

She tucks her hand back down to her side as she looks around for a chair to sit in. She won't find one. I don't keep chairs in my office. It invites people to stay and talk. I don't want to talk to people. If we are talking, that means we aren't working hard enough. And, if someone has something to say that is actually useful enough to listen to for longer than five to ten minutes, then that is what meeting rooms are for. Not my office.

"Um...Noah sent me in to meet you."

I rub my neck in annoyance. "And why did Noah want you to meet me?"

She frowns. "Because he said you would like to meet me. I'm his new assistant, and he said that we would be working closely together, so I should introduce myself."

I look at her. Really look at her. She's fresh out of college;

that much is obvious. This is probably her first job. She doesn't have a clue what she signed up for when she started working for my company. I give her a month, tops, before she decides I'm too much of an ass to bother working for. It takes tough people to work for me. You have to be able to take getting yelled at and not back down. You have to be willing to fight for what you believe in. She looks like, if I yelled at her, she'd run out of here, crying. Might as well get it over with. Rip off the Band-Aid, as some would say.

"Angela, you seem like a nice girl, but you must not have listened very carefully at orientation if you think that you are ever allowed to talk to me. You are Noah's assistant, not mine. If you have something that you need to tell me, you tell my assistant, Casey. You don't waste my time, trying to talk to me. You don't call me. You don't email me. You don't knock on my door. And you sure as hell don't come into my office for no other reason than to say hello. Got it?"

She bites her juicy red lip, and my mind immediately flashes back to the last woman I saw bite her lip like that.

*Skye.*

But, even when Skye wasn't wearing red lipstick, like this girl, her lip looked a million times more inviting than this woman's.

"Why haven't you left yet?" I half-yell, half-ask.

She releases her lip. "Sorry, Noah told me you'd most likely yell at me but to stay anyway, that it was good for you. That you would yell at me, but then you'd be nice. That you just needed to vent because you'd had a couple of bad weeks. He said to just wade through your storm of emotions, and then things would be a lot better. That you just needed someone to yell at who could take it, so then you could be nice."

I sigh. I'll deal with Noah later. "Please tell Noah to stop messing with me. It's not helpful. And you would do a lot better at this company if you stopped listening to everything that Noah told you to do."

She smiles, tucking her blonde hair behind her ear. "He said you would say that."

I run my hand through my thick hair, annoyed and frustrated. Noah's wrong if he thinks this is going to get my frustrations out. This is doing the opposite.

She puts her hand on mine. "The company is running well. Just try to relax. I'll see you soon, Brody." She removes her hand, turns, and walks out.

I blink rapidly, trying to figure out what the fuck just happened when another knock rattles against my door, but this time, the person doesn't wait for me to answer. Noah just strides in.

"Hey, boss," he says in his usual chipper self.

"What, Noah?" I want to yell at him for Angela, but that would mean more of my time was wasted.

He grins, folding his arms across his chest while he sits on the edge of my desk. "You fucked up the numbers again," he says.

I frown. "No, I didn't. That's not possible. I checked them three separate times."

He shakes his head and throws some papers on my desk.

I narrow my eyes as I pick up the stack of papers and stare at the numbers. I do the math in my head and can already tell that I'm way off. *Damn it.*

I throw them down in frustration, watching as they scatter everywhere.

Noah smirks and folds his arms across his chest like he's the shit and I'm an idiot. Even though he wouldn't have a job if it wasn't for me busting my balls every damn day for this company.

"Now, will you listen to me?" he asks, but it isn't meant to be a question.

"Why? I fucked up. It won't happen again."

He shakes his head. "Except it's happened almost every day since we got back from the Bahamas. That woman still has your dick obsessed with her."

"So what if she does? I don't use my dick to get work done."

He laughs. "You might as well. Your dick might do a better job than what you are currently doing."

I get up from my desk and walk over to the small window that stares out into Detroit below. I lean against the wall, looking out at the people walking around below.

"You need to do something about this. You need to get her out of your system, so you can focus on what's really important. The launch. We are launching our second video game in less than three weeks. We've done the unthinkable, raising billions of dollars when we have no money ourselves. We don't even pay ourselves enough to live off of. But, if we get this right, then the world will take us seriously, and we can actually start paying ourselves."

I nod. I know he's right. Although I don't care about money. I have a condo my uncle gave to me when he died. And what money I do earn, I spend on fast cars. I don't need anything else to keep me happy. What else could money buy me that I don't already have? I just enjoy creating. Working hard. That's what's in it for me.

"What do you suggest I do about it?"

He grins. "Fuck her."

I narrow my stare at him. "She lives hundreds of miles away from here in Albuquerque. I live in Detroit. It's not exactly easy for me to just go fuck her and then come back to work."

"I think it would be worth the weekend trip. But, if you don't think you can take the time off, I know an assistant who would be more than willing to help you out."

I cringe at that thought. "Really? She's barely twenty."

"So? I'm not telling you to fuck her for her brain or maturity. You haven't fucked anyone since Skye. You need to move on, get out there again."

"Get out of my office, and get back to work," I snap, done with this conversation.

Noah grins and walks out of my office without a word.

I'll decide when I fuck a woman and who she will be. Right now, I don't need the distraction. I'll just increase the difficulty of my workout tonight. That will get whatever this is that I'm feeling out of my system so that I can focus.

———

I open the door to my condo. It's late, as it always is when I get home from work. About a quarter after ten. Sometimes, I wonder why I don't just create an apartment for myself at the office. That way, I don't ever have to leave. I can spend every second being productive.

I walk toward the kitchen, not bothering to flick on the lights. I like it dark. I need to eat, exercise, and pass out. I don't need light for any of it.

I throw the fridge open to pull out the premade meals that I prepare myself once a week, so then I don't have to think about food the rest of the week when I see a shadow move.

I sigh as I pull out my container of food. I walk the three feet to the microwave, pop in the food, and hit the button for it to start.

"What are you doing here?" I ask without turning around. I don't want to look at her. I don't want to talk to her. I don't want her here.

"Noah said you needed some help with relaxing tonight," Angela says, walking up behind me and rubbing my shoulders.

I tense instead of relaxing.

The microwave finishes, and I pull my dinner out and walk over to the bar where there is only one barstool. I take a seat, ignoring her. I begin eating my grilled chicken and steamed vegetables.

She tries to push her body onto my lap, but I don't let her. I just keep eating like I always do by myself.

I'm going to kill Noah. He should know better than to think he can have any control over my life.

"You need to go," I say sternly, still not looking at her.

"I don't think that's what you really want."

I frown and finally look at her. "You have no idea what I want."

She bites her fingernail and looks at me as she cocks her head, like by studying me, she is going to figure out what I want.

"Maybe not, but I know what all men want." She reaches around and pulls on the tie holding her wrap dress closed. The dress falls open, and then she shrugs her shoulders as the dress falls to the floor.

My eyes burn into her black lace bra and thong underwear. She has a gorgeous body. And she's right; I'm a man in need of fucking a woman's brains out. The only reason I'm fighting it at all is that I hate when Noah is right. It will only empower him to pull shit like this again.

"Wait for me in my bedroom, down the hallway to the right." She smiles.

"And, if you tell Noah about this, you're fired."

9

————

**SKYE**

MY HANDS CONTINUE to do compressions over the small puppy's chest. I'm exhausted. I've been trying to save this puppy for three hours now.

Most vets would have given up a long time ago. He was hit by a car, and most of the bones in his body are broken. He has internal bleeding that I know I can't stop. And he's been touch and go since he arrived.

But he's a fighter, and I won't give up on him. So, I keep doing compressions, trying to convince his heart to keep beating.

"Skye," Alicia, my vet technician, says in a stern voice.

I keep pumping my arms over the puppy's small chest.

"Skye, it's time," she says, placing her hand on my shoulder.

I know she's right. That he's already gone. But, for some reason, it's harder for me to give up on the strays than the ones who have an owner. At least the ones with an owner had a good life. They were loved.

This puppy grew up alone. He's barely eight months, and if the car accident hadn't taken his life, starvation most likely would have.

"Time of death: six thirty-three," I say, stopping the compressions.

I stroke his head. This is the hardest part of the job—when I can't save them. This is what I was put on this earth to do, and when I fail, I'm lost.

"You should go home. You weren't even supposed to be on duty today," Alicia says.

I nod. I'll go. I'm too exhausted to be of any use here.

I walk like a zombie to my office to collect my things, and then I start walking the half-mile down the road to the small farmhouse that I call home.

Usually, I like the walk. It gives me time to clear my head before I'm greeted by my herd of animals. But not today. Today, I don't want to think. Today is hard.

My thoughts go back to the beach. To Brody, as they often have these last couple of months since I returned from my vacation. And I feel the familiar feeling of anger take over. It's easy than the pain I feel when I think about the puppy that I couldn't save. A puppy that didn't even have a name.

I open the door to my small farmhouse and am greeted by my four mutt dogs. "Hey, Sherbet, Grumpy, Ernie, and Lady," I say, greeting each dog.

I try to smile, but I just can't today. Even Ernie's infectious grin isn't enough to warm my heart. Not today.

I walk the few feet to the back door and open the door to let them out into the backyard. I might be exhausted, but my day doesn't end when I come home. I have three horses, two cows, six chickens, three pigs, a rooster, four dogs, and three cats that rely on me. So, I follow the dogs out into the yard and get to work. Thankful to have something to keep my mind occupied instead of my lonely thoughts.

The sun is setting fast by the time I'm about finished feeding and giving the animals the attention they need. I start walking back up the field toward the house to make myself something to eat with the dogs fast on my heels, excited that it's time for them to get fed as well.

I sense him before I see him. My body is used to being alert for when I feel danger nearby.

"You're not welcome here," I say, grabbing on to Grumpy and giving the rest of the dogs a look to stay by me.

They all do, sitting carefully next to me as they intently stare at the stranger.

Brody is standing just outside the fence on my property. His face is clean-shaven, and his hair is shorter than the last time I saw him. In a dark suit, he's very out of place here.

"I just want to talk. Can I take you to a late dinner or to get a drink or something?"

"No," I say as I continue to hold on to Grumpy, the only dog I have that isn't fully trained yet. My negative energy transfers through my body to his, the longer I hold him, getting him even more worked up as he fights to try to get to the intruder.

Brody looks down at the dog I'm holding on to. "He friendly?" he asks as he puts his hand on the gate.

"No, he's not friendly. Especially toward men he feels are intruders." I let him jump forward a little bit in my hands as I continue to hold on to him. He growls fiercely, making Brody hesitate.

Brody frowns. "What would it take to get you to talk to me?"

I laugh deviously. "There is nothing you could do to get me to talk to you."

"I hurt you that bad, huh?"

"No, I just don't give a shit about you. You aren't even supposed to be here. You were supposed to be out of my life after the week, remember?"

"I didn't get my last fuck in."

"And whose fault is that?"

"Yours."

I raise an eyebrow. "Seriously? It wasn't my fault. It was yours! You were the one who said you would come to the airport and didn't. It seems you got your last fuck in just fine, just not with me."

He grins. "So, you do care."

"No," I lie.

"You were the one who went running home to Gabe. You were the one who cut our time short." He looks at the dogs. "So, which one is Gabe anyway?"

My eyes darken. He thinks Gabe is one of my animals. Now, it's my turn to hurt him.

"This is Grumpy. That's Ernie, Sherbet, and Lady."

He frowns. "So, Gabe is a cat."

"Tommy, Jordan, and Ruffus."

"A horse?"

"Blondie, Pumpkin, and Sandy."

"The other animals?"

I smile. "Nope."

He runs his hand through his short hair before rubbing his neck. "You aren't going to tell me who Gabe is, are you?"

"Not likely, no. I like that you have too many thoughts going through your head right now as you try to figure it out. And it's driving you crazy."

He smirks. "It's not driving me crazy. Not having your mouth sucking my cock—that is what is driving me crazy. I just want to know who Gabe is, so I know when to duck when he takes a swing at me."

"That's not happening."

"Which part? Because I guarantee that your lips are going to be wrapped around my dick by the end of the night."

I shake my head. "You're still so cocky, aren't you? We are done. I don't want anything to do with you."

"You sure about that? Because your body is telling me differently."

I glare at him. "We are done."

He reaches for the gate and opens it, thinking now is his opportunity to walk inside and catch me off guard. I'm sure he thinks, if he can get close enough where I can smell his cologne again, close enough that I can see his charming dimples, close enough that I can hear his beating heart, then I'll change my mind. I'll just fall back into his arms again, just like we were back on the beach in our fantasy world. That bubble burst the second he sent me the text message with the big-tits woman.

"Don't take another step forward!" I shout.

He doesn't listen. I release Grumpy and release the rest of the dogs with a look. I just wish, for once, they were actually capable of attacking a man when I needed them to. Instead, they run over and attack him all right. Just with kisses and hugs and tail wags.

But it gets the job done. He can't move, and I take the opportunity to run inside. I slam the door shut and lock it tightly behind me as I lean against the door. *Can this day get any worse?*

10

———

**BRODY**

God, how I've missed her.

I've missed her sass.

I've missed her wit.

I've missed her charm.

Her smile, body, intelligence, fierceness. Everything. I've missed everything.

Except, now, she hates my guts. I knew sending her that text message would bite me in the ass one day.

I look down at the dogs that are jumping all over me. Slobbering and getting hair all over my suit. I'm not a dog person or an animal person of any kind really. I could be, I guess. But I've never spent any time with them or thought I needed to have an animal in my life. I prefer my alone time in peace rather than having to take care of another living thing.

So, I have no idea how to get them to stop. I slowly back up toward the gate and manage to wiggle out without letting the beasts loose.

I take a deep breath as I walk back to the car I rented and move on to plan B. She clearly isn't happy to see me, but I do know her weaknesses, what she won't turn down.

I open the back door and pull out the bottle of tequila and Chinese takeout. I put on my most charming grin as I walk back to her front door and knock loudly.

I wait, knowing that she's going to be stubborn and not want to open the door. But a few minutes pass, and she slowly relents, coming to the door.

"I brought food and tequila because I'm sure you don't have any food in the house," I say even though I don't know if that's true. I just know that she cares about her animals more than she does herself. That's clear from where I sat in my car, watching her before I got out.

I stare at her more closely, getting a good look at the changes since the last time I saw her months ago. Her hair is pulled back, but it no longer has the blue streaks that ran through her hair before. Her hair is no longer jet-black either; it's more a medium brown. Most of her piercings are no longer covering her face. The tattoos are hidden by her long sleeves underneath her scrubs even though it's the middle of summer.

Her eyes are what give me the most concern though. People change their appearance. Maybe she was going through a rebel phase that she's trying to get past now. But her eyes are expelling a sadness that I've never seen before. Maybe this is the same sadness that she was running from on vacation. Whatever is in her eyes is what she needed me to fuck away and make her forget. Now that I'm gone, the reality of that pain is back.

She opens the door just a little and snatches the food and alcohol out of my hand. Then, she slams the door in my face before I have a chance to push my way inside. Not that I would. I like control, but I would never make her feel unsafe.

I sigh. On to plan C. I walk back to my car and drive the half-mile back to the clinic where my new favorite vet tech, Alicia, is.

"No luck, huh?" she asks when I step back inside.

"Nope, but I have a plan C. And, if that doesn't work, I'll try plan D and so on."

She smiles. "And you want my help?"

I nod.

"I shouldn't help you, but Skye doesn't need to be alone tonight. She could use some company even if it's bad company."

I frown. "I'm not bad company."

"Skye told me what you did in the Bahamas."

"Fine. I'm not the best. But I do know I'm a good distraction, and it seems Skye is in need of a distraction." I bat my eyes at her while saying, "Please."

"If you bring her a sick animal to take care of, she will let you in."

I grin. "That was exactly what I was thinking."

"Hold on," she says, disappearing into the back room and then reappearing with a cardboard box with small holes cut out on the top.

I take the box from her and open the lid. I jump back, dropping the box.

She does a full-belly laugh, grabbing her stomach as she walks over and picks up the box that I just dropped.

"Is this a joke? Did you and Skye plan this to get back at me?" I ask, my voice much higher than usual.

Alicia continues to laugh as she walks the box back over to me. "No, it's not a joke. The snake needs medical attention."

I frown. "I'm not a big fan of snakes."

"I would have never guessed that," she snarks.

"Why can't I bring a puppy or kitten or something that needs her help?"

"One, because most of our puppies and kittens need more medical help than what she can provide at her house. And, two, because I'm still not a huge fan of yours, and I want to make you suffer as much as possible. Consider it my own personal test to see if you are worthy of hanging out with my friend." She holds the box out to me. "Now, do you want to see Skye tonight or not?"

I slowly take the box. I'll just keep the lid on the whole time. I'm not sure if a sick snake is enough to get Skye to let me into her house, but I'll give it a try. If not, I'll come back and find the cutest puppy to take back and try again.

"So, you want to tell me about Gabe?" I ask.

She smirks. "Nope, I'm not touching that conversation. If Skye wants to tell you, she will."

"Thanks," I say, holding up the box a little as I walk toward the door.

"But, if I were you, I wouldn't mention Gabe tonight. She's been through enough tonight, so don't add to her depression."

I nod. *Too late*, I think.

But I'll table the Gabe questions until later. It seems that no one wants to tell me exactly who Gabe is, but I have enough resources that I'm sure I can figure it out if I put some of my guys on it.

I put the box with the snake in the passenger seat next to me, and then I climb in the driver's seat and drive back to Skye's place, keeping my eye on the box the whole time, making sure the snake doesn't slither out. I park the car on the gravel driveway in front of her house, behind an old pickup truck that doesn't look like it has run in ten years at least.

I climb out of the car and walk around to the passenger side. I take the box out, carrying it with both hands as I walk up the gravel driveway to the front of the white farmhouse. It's not very large and much older than any house I've ever been in besides my grandparents'. There are daisies planted outside the red front door. The house is not that big, which surprises me after how much money she spent on vacation. I figured she would have a mansion somewhere. She owns what seems like quite a bit of land, but that still wouldn't cost as much as a nice house would.

I knock on the red door that needs a new coat of paint and wait to see if Skye will open the door or at least respond. I knock again after a few seconds pass. I hear stomping footsteps inside, and finally, she creaks the door open just enough to see me.

"What do you want, Brody?"

I hold up the box. "I have a sick snake that needs your veterinarian skills."

She glares at me as she slowly opens the door. "Well, let's see it," she says, exhaling deeply.

I grin and lift the lid just enough so that she can see inside.

Her gaze darts from inside the box to me. "There isn't a snake in that box."

"Will you just take a look at the snake? I'm not sure if it is sick or not, but I'm concerned."

"I would, but there is no snake in the box."

I throw the lid open and find the box empty. "Shit."

I run back to my rental car and peek into the windows, not daring to open it.

Skye walks slowly over to the car and looks in the window. "Was there ever really a snake, or is this all some stupid hoax where you try to save me from the snake or something?"

"There was really a snake. Alicia helped me out." I hesitantly look over at Skye.

She shakes her head as she tucks a loose strand behind her ear. "Alicia needs to mind her own business."

"She's just looking out for you. She said she was concerned after what happened today."

She looks up at me. "She told you?"

"No, she just told me you had a rough day and to treat you well. That you needed a distraction."

She stares at me for a moment, lost in thought, and then

returns her gaze to the car. "There," she says, pointing to the driver's side of the car where I'm standing.

I stare at the snake as it slithers up the side of the seat. I have no idea how we are going to capture it. "Should we call animal control or something?"

She laughs. "You're afraid of the snake, aren't you?"

"No."

"Then, reach in, and grab the snake just behind the base of the head."

I frown. "No, it could kill me if it bites me."

"It's not venomous. And it's sick, so its reflexes are much slower. It shouldn't be a problem at all."

I stare at the snake that seems to be taunting me. There is no way I'm reaching in and grabbing that snake. I don't care if my masculinity is put into question. Me and snakes don't get along.

Skye rolls her eyes and then throws open the passenger door. She sticks her upper body in, and the next thing I know, she's holding on to the snake and carrying it into her house.

*Superwoman. She's fucking superwoman.*

I follow after her as she walks into the house, not asking for permission to come in because I don't want to know the answer. As soon as I step inside the small house, I'm greeted again by her four dogs jumping and licking me.

"Down," Skye commands.

All but one listen to her. She gives the last one a stern look, and he eventually stops jumping on me as well.

Skye lays the snake out on the counter and starts examining it while I step cautiously into the kitchen to watch her work. She runs her hands over the snake, like it's a dog or a cat.

"It just has a cold. I'll give her some medications, and she'll be feeling better by tomorrow." She looks at me. "Can you get me the box?"

I frown as I carry the box from the front porch to her. "Don't you think we should put it in something more secure? It already escaped once."

"How did I not realize how much of a pansy you were?" she asks, putting the snake into the box.

I smirk. "Probably because you were too busy getting your brains fucked out to care."

She puts her hands on her hips. "What are you doing here?"

"Isn't it obvious?"

"No, it's not." She walks back to the living room where there is an empty bowl that used to contain her Chinese food and a glass filled with tequila. She takes a seat on the worn-in tan couch. Her dogs climb up next to her, making themselves at home as they curl up with her and each other.

I take a seat on the reclining chair next to the couch, knowing that she isn't going to offer me food or drink. She doesn't want me here, so why would she make it more comfortable for me to be here?

"I want our last fuck."

"You know that's not going to happen. You knew before you came here that I would never give it to you. That, even if you had treated me like a perfect gentleman that last day, I still wouldn't fuck you after you showed up here. I told you, I was only ever interested in one week."

She takes a drink of her tequila, and I watch as it slides down her throat.

"I wanted to make sure you were okay," I say as my eyes burn into hers.

"You don't care about me."

I sigh. "You're right. I only care about you as long as I get to fuck you, but it seems you won't let me fuck you until I pretend to care, so you can see my predicament."

"I'm not talking about Gabe."

"I didn't ask about Gabe. I want to know why you are in so

much pain right now. And don't lie to me. I know your body better than anyone. I know that your eyes are usually filled with a little bit of light, but today, they only see the darkness. Your breathing is slow and heavy, like the weight of today is pushing you down, making it hard to move, let alone breathe. Why are you in such pain?"

She stares off into space, giving me no indication if she is going to talk to me or not. "Because bad things happen to creatures that don't deserve it."

I narrow my eyes, not understanding.

"I lost a dog tonight. It was painful. He was just a puppy. He didn't deserve to die, but there was nothing I could do."

She drinks the rest of the tequila. She shakes the glass, listening as the ice rattles around.

"I'm sorry," I say because that's all I can say.

"Life sucks."

I nod and walk back to the kitchen to get the tequila. I grab the bottle and bring it back to her. She takes it from me and pours herself easily three more shots' worth. She's drunk already and getting drunker by the minute.

I don't stop her. She needs the distraction. And, since she won't take me up on my offer to let me fuck away the pain, the alcohol is the only thing that will do.

She keeps talking about how the poor puppy didn't deserve to die. That he didn't deserve the life he was given. But, as sad as it is that she lost the puppy, it's not what she's really sad about. There is still something that she isn't telling me. Something that I'm desperate to know. Because the only way I'll get to fuck her again is if she gets past whatever darkness is currently consuming her.

## 11

# SKYE

I GET a lick on my face, as I almost always do when it's time to get up in the morning. I open my eyes and sit up in bed. I feel like I was hit by a truck, and then that truck backed up and ran me over again.

*How much did I drink last night?*

I feel my stomach heaving, and I run, making it to the toilet just in time for the alcohol to all start coming back up. Apparently, I drank way too much.

I sit on the cold floor for a minute before I stand and clean my mouth out with water and brush my teeth. I vaguely remember the pain. I remember the tequila. And I remember Brody.

*Ugh, why did he have to come back into my life?*

He's a giant dick, but he's a dick that I want to ride. And, even though I can't deal with him right now, he's all I'm going to be able to think about until he leaves town. Maybe I can just fuck him once like he wants, and then he will leave.

I doubt it, but maybe the sex will suck, and I'll realize that what we had in the Bahamas was just a fantasy that I played up in my head. It wasn't real.

I take a deep breath and get a whiff of what smells like pancakes. Except it can't be. I don't live with anyone else. I must be dreaming.

I walk out into my living area, and the smell gets stronger. I'm greeted by my dogs and cats, which I give each of them some attention before rounding the corner and continuing into my kitchen.

My stomach flips at the sight of Brody cooking shirtless in my kitchen. Of course, he stayed. And of course, my body doesn't understand that it shouldn't get excited about backstabbers like Brody, no matter how hot they are.

"You know how to cook?" I ask, surprised.

He turns his head as he continues to stand in front of my stove. "I have many talents. Cooking isn't one of them, but I can make a basic meal."

I want to yell at him to get out, but I really want the pancakes. My stomach is aching for some carbs to soak up the alcohol still causing havoc in my stomach.

"Sit down," he commands.

I walk over to my two-seater kitchen table and take a seat. I don't have the strength to argue with him.

He brings me a large glass of water and Advil.

I take the water and drink until the glass is completely empty.

"I made you a Bloody Mary, too. Not sure if you want it though, but it might help to fight the hangover with a little more alcohol."

I stare at the glass; there is no way I can drink it.

"Nope, I'm good," I say, scrunching my nose up at the sight.

He grins, and my heart melts a little at the sight of his dimples.

"The pancakes should help," he says, placing a large plate of pancakes drenched in syrup in front of me.

I dig in without a thank-you. He's the reason I drank too much last night anyway. He provided the alcohol. He amplified my emotions by coming here.

He watches me as I eat while he does dishes at the sink. I continue to eat while discreetly looking around at my house. It's clean. Like really, really clean. The dog and cat hair has been swept off the floor. The counters and end tables are dusted and clean. The clutter of mail I usually leave scattered on the counter is now sitting in an organized pile. The dog toys have been picked up and placed in a basket. And he's not only washed the dishes he created but the dishes from yesterday as well.

I put my fork down as my stomach finally starts to feel better.

"What are you doing?" I ask.

"Dishes."

"No, why did you clean up my house?"

"Because, despite what you think about me, I can be a nice guy if I want to."

"No, you're a dick. You would only ever be a nice guy in order to get something. What do you want?"

He tosses the dish towel he was using to dry the dishes down onto the counter next to the sink.

"I would think it's obvious." His eyes show a desire that takes over his entire body.

I roll my eyes, trying to act like I can easily just forget about him. That nothing he does affects me. Not his stare. Not his muscular body. Not his intense grin. Nothing can touch me.

But he knows my body too well. He knows it's all a lie.

He pulls out the chair across from me and casually sits down, his legs spread and his body leaning back in the chair like he owns it.

Grumpy walks over to Brody and licks him on his arm. Brody gently pets his head.

I frown, staring at my dog that hates everybody. He hates Alicia and everyone else from work. He hates Gabe. He hates strangers. He won't go near them, except to bark. Not Brody, though. Apparently, he's decided, the one person he should hate the most, he actually likes. I'll have to talk to Grumpy later.

"I have a proposition for you," he says.

I take a bite of my pancake so that I can answer him with my mouth full. Maybe, if I'm as disgusting as possible, he won't want anything to do with me. "Let's hear it then."

He watches my mouth as I talk, but it seems to just get him more excited.

"I want to continue our arrangement from before."

"For how long?" I ask before I realize what I'm doing.

He grins and cocks his head from side to side, like this is way easier than he thought it was going to be.

I shouldn't have given him any indication that I was interested in continuing our arrangement. I should have just said no right away. But my big mouth always seems to get me into trouble.

"You tell me. You owe me at least one more day, but I don't think you want to stop at just one more day. I'm good with another day, a week, a year. What do you want, baby?"

I hate how he speaks like he already knows the answer to the question that he is asking. He thinks I'm going to say I want a year. But I won't give him the satisfaction of being right.

"You think you can come here, clean up my house a bit, and make me breakfast, and then all is forgiven, huh?" I grin, taking another bite of my pancake.

"I didn't think I needed forgiveness because you don't give a shit about me."

I narrow my eyes, glaring at him. "You're right. I don't. But

I've had enough pricks in my life to know that the only thing to do with them is throw them out with the trash, not make arrangements that only benefit one side."

I get up from the table and walk to my bedroom. I pull out a suitcase and start throwing clothes into it.

I continue to throw clothes into my suitcase, not bothering to look at what I'm throwing in until the suitcase is filled with clothes. I can't think straight. All I can think about is that Brody wants to have sex with me again. And, despite the pain that it will likely cause me, I want to fuck him again, too. But I can't. I walk a few feet to my small bathroom and grab my already-packed toiletry bag from my last trip to LA. I toss it into my suitcase. I have to sit on the suitcase to get it to close.

Then, I look into my closet and find a pair of jeans and a T-shirt. I put them on and pull my hair up into a ponytail. I give myself a quick glance in the mirror and then grab my suitcase. I walk out of the bedroom, carrying my suitcase, hoping that Brody will get the hint and just leave me alone.

"What are you doing?"

I don't look at him. If I look at him again, I'll just start drooling over his shirtless, hard body. I'll start remembering how good it felt to have his strong arms wrapped around me and how good it felt to lick every inch of his chest. I'll start caving, and I can't afford to cave.

"I have a flight to catch. Don't worry about the animals. I have a babysitter coming in a few hours to watch them. But make sure you take the snake back to the clinic."

I walk to the door and throw it open, pulling my suitcase out behind me. The door slams shut behind me. I don't say good-bye to my animals, and I definitely don't say good-bye to Brody. If I spend one more second in the house, I might stay instead of leaving.

I walk to my truck and throw the suitcase in the back. I start it up and drive off. Only when I've driven a few miles away do I allow myself to look into the rearview mirror. He's not behind me as much as I wish on some level that he were. I could really use some distraction even if I can't do his arrangement. It's wrong in more ways than one.

**12**

———

**BRODY**

I DON'T KNOW if she really has a flight to catch or if she just packed and left in an attempt to get rid of me. But it won't work.

I look at the box that hopefully still contains the snake as I grab my shirt and push it back on before I pick up the box and dart out the door behind Skye. I get a glimpse of Skye's pickup truck driving off down the road in the general direction of the airport. I want to jump in my rental and chase after her, ensuring that she's going to the airport. I would if it wasn't for this damn snake.

I throw open the trunk of my car and place the box with the snake in it, keeping it as far away from me as possible. I slam the trunk and hop in the driver's seat. I speed off down the road as fast as I possibly can. When I get there, I carry the box inside and hand it off to the receptionist, not bothering to wait for Alicia to come get it. I make the receptionist verify that the snake is still in the box and not in my car before I leave, but that's all I wait for.

And then I'm back in my car, racing toward the airport, hoping that she didn't lie to me and that I manage to stop her or at least get on the same flight with her.

Thank God for checked bags because that's where I find her waiting in line—to check her bag. I watch her from a distance so that she won't know I'm here. She's oblivious to me as she stands in the line. And it gives me another opportunity to really just watch her. She looks so different from the last time I saw her in the Bahamas. She looked so normal compared to now. Now, she's trying to blend in instead of stand out.

She finishes at the counter, and I immediately go up after her. Luckily, there is a young woman working there. With a little flirting, I get her to tell me exactly where Skye is headed—LA. And there just so happens to be several seats left on the same flight as her, so I buy a ticket. I could try to convince her to stay here and think more about my offer. But I doubt she would consider staying. This way, I get to find out more about her life and what she'll be doing in LA.

The flight attendant calls for boarding, and Skye gets in line while I linger back. She still hasn't noticed me, but I do know that I will be sitting about three rows behind her on the plane. I give her about a fifty-fifty shot whether she will see me or not.

I board the plane and immediately spot her six rows back, fumbling with her phone. I doubt she'll even notice that I'm on the plane, which will give me the entire flight to plan on how I want to reveal to her that I followed her to LA.

As I start walking by her, she looks up. Her eyes widen as she realizes what's happening. She opens her mouth to say something but doesn't get it out before I casually walk past her and take my seat.

I smirk but otherwise don't give her any attention. This is better. Now, she's going to have the entire flight to worry about me.

I put my earbuds in, planning on listening to an audiobook about business strategies to keep my mind occupied. I close my eyes, ignoring the safety briefing and all the other BS that happens before the flight takes off. I've flown enough times to know how everything works. I feel the plane take off at some point while I listen to my book.

"Excuse me," I hear Skye's voice say even through my haze of sleep and the audiobook.

I try to ignore her as she convinces the stranger next to me to swap seats with her. I keep my eyes closed like I don't notice her at all as she finally takes a seat next to me, even after her thigh and hand brush against my leg—whether intentionally or unintentionally. I try to act like I couldn't care less about her when what I really want to do is sneak her into the restroom and fuck her brains out.

"I know you can hear me and that you know I'm here. Stop acting like you can't hear me," Skye says.

"Oh, I didn't realize you were on this plane." I remove one of my earbuds, giving her half of my attention.

"Don't play dumb," she says, reaching for my other earbud and jerking it out of my ear.

"I knew you couldn't get enough of me."

She huffs and rolls her eyes again. She lifts her legs up into her seat, and she wraps her arms around them like she is giving herself one big hug. "Why did you follow me here?"

"I didn't follow you. I live in LA. When you told me you were leaving, I got on the next available flight since there was no longer a reason to stay in Albuquerque."

"Liar. You don't live in LA."

I closely study her. "You looked me up, did you?"

She looks away from me. "No, I didn't."

I laugh. "You totally did."

"No, I didn't," she says empathetically.

"Then, how do you know I don't live in LA?"

"Because you live in Detroit."

I bite my lip to keep my excitement down. She looked me up.

She wants me just as badly as I want her. I just have to figure out what the key is to unlocking her hesitation about starting this up again. Because, clearly, the pain I caused her on the last day in paradise isn't the reason.

"Why don't you want to do the arrangement?"

"Because you're an ass."

"I am, but then that's exactly what you wanted. An ass. So, tell me the real reason you won't agree to my arrangement, and I'll leave you alone forever."

"For real? After I tell you the truth, you'll get out of my life and never come back?"

"I promise I'll leave you alone. If that's what you want."

She leans her chair back and closes her eyes like she's going to take a long nap.

"Are you going to tell me or not?"

"I'm going to show you."

———

To my surprise, the rest of the flight is uneventful. We both sleep —or at least pretend to sleep. When we land, we get off the flight, being relatively civil to one another. After we collect our bags, she tells me to get into her car with her.

I do.

The Maserati we climb into isn't a rental. It's a car that she owns but is the complete opposite of her car in Albuquerque. That pickup truck was all about function and getting the job done with no fuss about its appearance. This car is a luxury car with little purpose other than to provide comfort and be flashy to all those who look at it.

"Do you have a split personality or something?" I ask as she drives.

"No."

"Then, explain to me why you have such a fancy car in LA and such a shitty one in Albuquerque."

She glares at me. "My truck isn't shitty."

I raise my eyebrows.

"Just because it isn't what you expect on the outside doesn't mean it isn't worthy on the inside."

"That was deep."

"Just shut up until we get to my condo."

"Is your condo as fancy as this car? Because I have a feeling that your house back in Albuquerque is going to feel run-down compared to your condo here."

She turns a little too fast around the next corner, and I hit my head on the roof of the car.

She smirks. "Like I said, you should probably just stop talking until we get to my condo."

I do but only because, clearly, she won't tell me anything until we get to her condo. Something at her condo holds the key to everything she's been hiding from me. She thinks she's going to be able to get rid of me once we are there, but I don't think there is anything she can show me that will make me want to leave. And all I have to do is get one kiss, and she'll be begging me for more.

Skye parks the car in a fancy parking garage and then makes her way to the elevator. Of course, she presses the button for the top floor. I smirk at her, guessing that her friend paid for this place while Skye pays for her house back home. I just don't know which version she'd rather be, not that it matters. I'd fuck her either way.

The elevators doors open, and she stomps out like she can't get out of there fast enough. I follow, making sure to walk as close as possible behind her to be as obnoxious as I can. She pulls a key out of her purse and unlocks the door, gesturing for me to follow her inside. I do, letting the door close behind me. I watch as a tall man with light-colored hair in a business suit greets her. He wraps her in his arms and firmly kisses her on the lips.

I glare at the man who has my woman wrapped in his arms. My woman's lips pressed against his. A few moments pass before he finally comes up for air. Just enough time for my internal rage to fill every crevice inside me.

"Baby, this is Brody, the man I told you about from my Bahamas vacation. Brody, this is Gabe, my fiancé."

Gabe extends his hand to me. I take it, gripping as firmly as I can.

"It's nice to finally meet you, Brody," Gabe says.

"You, too."

He squeezes Skye one more time with a bright smile on his face, happy to have his fiancée home. She, on the other hand, couldn't seem more uncomfortable in his arms. The only reason she even has a smile on her face is that she can show me that I was wrong. That our relationship is over.

"I hate this, but I have to run. I have a meeting I have to get to. But we should all do dinner tonight," Gabe says, kissing Skye one more time on the lips before giving me a nod and slipping out of the condo.

I'm not sure I believe that the relationship is real. She probably just called an old friend and asked him to pretend to be her fiancé to try to get rid of me. But whatever it is, I'm going to figure it out.

"What the fuck is going on?"

## 13

## SKYE

"THAT ISN'T YOUR FIANCÉ," Brody says.

"Are you serious? Gabe is my fiancé. He told you so himself without any probing from me. We kissed. We share this condo together. What more proof do you need?" I say, my voice loud and angry.

I thought he would've stormed out the second he found out I had a fiancé, but apparently, he doesn't believe anything I tell him is true, so I don't even know why I bother trying to explain.

"I need a heck of a lot more proof than that. You didn't even want to kiss him. How can you be engaged to a person and not even want to kiss him?"

"Just because you fucked me for a week in the Bahamas doesn't mean you know me. You have no idea why I reacted the way that I did to Gabe kissing me."

Brody starts walking around the condo, his eyes traveling over everything he can find. He opens doors, sticking his head inside, only to reemerge.

"What are you doing?" I ask, walking behind him.

"I'm looking for proof."

I exhale deeply. "You promised you would leave after I told you the truth about why I wouldn't agree to your arrangement."

"I said I would leave after you told me the truth. I'm not sure you've told me the truth yet."

He walks around our living room, staring at the white and light-gray massive walls that take up almost two stories with a few large pieces of artwork. He raises an eyebrow at me as he walks down the hallway to the bedroom that Gabe and I share, which is also decorated in gray and white.

"Nope, I don't believe you."

I frown. "And why don't you believe me?"

I need him to believe me. I need him to leave. He knows enough. He can't stay and have dinner with us tonight. He'll find out far too much that I don't want him to know.

"Because I haven't found a single picture of you and your fiancé together in this entire condo. Not one single image." He walks to the closet and throws the door open, peeking inside. "Because, despite the fact that you say you live here, there are less than a dozen pieces of clothing of yours in this closet. Because, despite having a fiancé who lives in LA, you still have a home in Albuquerque along with a whole slew of animals, not to mention your veterinarian clinic. You claim to have a fiancé, yet you fuck me on a vacation without him less than six months ago. You claim to have a fiancé, yet you have no ring."

I look down at my bare hand as a tiny bit of hope creeps up inside me. I run into the bathroom and pull out the engagement box out of the top drawer. I open the box and pull out the large square diamond ring, which is easily four carats in size. I place it back on my hand after having not worn it for the past two weeks, and then I race back to the bedroom, holding out my hand to Brody.

"You're wrong. I have a ring."

Brody eyes the large diamond on my finger with suspicion. "How do I know that's not a fake?"

I roll my eyes. "Does it look like a fake?"

He cocks his head from side to side as he stares at it. "How would I know? I'm not a diamond expert."

"It's not a fake. Does it look like Gabe can't afford to buy me a nice diamond?" I hold my hands out to my sides, pointing at all the nice things in the condo that we share together.

"No, I'm sure Gabe could afford to buy you that ring. How do I know it's an engagement ring and not just a ring he bought for a close friend?"

"Really?"

"Fine, it looks like an engagement ring. But, if you're engaged, why weren't you wearing it? Why was it in a box here instead of on your finger in Albuquerque?"

"Because we want to keep our engagement private. Gabe is pretty well known out here, and I want to keep it out of the tabloids as long as we can."

He narrows his eyes. "So, you don't ever wear your ring in public?"

"No."

"When? When did he propose?"

I bite my lip and look away from him. I really don't want to answer him.

He chuckles. "You can't even come up with a quick story of how he proposed."

"He proposed to me the night I got back from the Bahamas. We weren't on the best of terms, which is why I went on vacation. I wanted to get some clarity on what I wanted when I returned. I came home when I found out he'd been in a motorcycle accident. I'd never been so scared in my life. I realized what a mistake I'd made. He got down on one knee and proposed in his hospital room despite being beaten up pretty badly. I said yes and haven't hesitated since."

He just stands there, staring at me, processing.

I sigh.

And then he suddenly starts moving. He walks out of the bedroom while I follow after him, curious if I finally said the thing that will make him leave. He doesn't walk toward the front door though. Instead, he walks into the kitchen, finds the bar, and starts digging through the alcohol. He shakes his head.

"What?" I snap.

He pulls out a decanter of whiskey and two glasses pouring us both a glass of alcohol from the decanter. He hands one of the glasses to me, and I take it, happy to have alcohol to finish this conversation. I need the strength to say anything to get him to leave.

"The bastard doesn't even have any tequila. So, you want to explain to me again how this is true love."

I don't answer him. It doesn't matter, and whatever excuse I make for him, it's clear that Brody won't believe me anyway.

Brody opens the door to the balcony and steps outside. I step out as well, happy to get some fresh air.

"Why?"

"Why else do you get married? Love."

"Why did you cheat on him? If you are so in love with him that you said yes the second you came back, why did you sleep with me?" He stares at me as he asks the question, like it's the most important question that he needs to know the answer to. His eyes seem sincere for the first time in a long time.

"Because it wasn't cheating."

I watch Brody's hands drum against the railing, and I want nothing more than for him to take me in his arms and kiss me. I want him to stroke my face. Or even just hold my hand. But it seems that he won't. But he has more self-control than I could've ever imagined while I'm on the edge of doing something very, very stupid.

"Were you on a break? Broken up? Is that why it wasn't technically cheating?"

"It wasn't cheating because we were never together."

Brody reaches out and grabs my hand, jerking me to him. My breathing is fast and heavy, as I'm filled with the weight of what I want him to do but can't let him.

"You're telling me that, after spending a week with me giving you the best sex of your life, you cut that short so that you could go back to marry a man you hadn't even kissed before?"

Pain—that's what I see when I look into Brody's eyes. It can't be pain though because I was nothing but a sex toy to him for the week. So, it must be something else. It must be that I heard him wrong, or it's jealousy at letting another man take the woman he was just with.

"We had kissed once, but that was it. I didn't think it was going anywhere."

He lets me go and takes a step back. "It must be love then."

My heart aches as he says the words, dripping with the same pain that I myself feel. It doesn't make sense for either of us to be feeling such pain, but it's how I feel.

"So, you'll leave then? I told you the truth. I told you that I wouldn't sleep with you again. And, just as I promised you, you can't stay."

He grins just enough for me to be concerned. "I think I'd like to have that dinner first. It's clear that he's rich, so I'm sure he knows where to get a good meal in town. And I'd like to hear from him a little more about how he got a woman like you to fall so quickly in love. I might need to use the skills myself someday. I'll leave after dinner if that's what you still want."

He says he will leave, but it seems more like a threat. I failed at getting him to leave once. I won't fail again.

# 14

## BRODY

She has a fucking fiancé. A wealthy, powerful, good-looking fiancé. A fiancé who has one of the sickest condos I've ever seen or had the privilege of being inside.

She has this whole other life in Albuquerque, which is completely different than their life here in LA. And I can't make the two lives, the two parts of her, make sense together in my head.

On the one hand, she's such a simple country girl who doesn't care about fancy things or if she fits into society; she only cares about her animals. She cares about doing good in the world, in leaving the world a better place than she found it.

But there's this other side of her. One that enjoys the finer things in life. Expensive vacations, fancy condos, and fast cars. The ring he gave her easily cost more than the wealth of several small countries.

She has two lives. Two worlds. And I don't think I'll be able to fit into either one of them. Because she's in love with the damn fiancé.

Or maybe she's lying. I've definitely seen her give warmer greetings before, and the answers to a lot of my questions didn't make sense. But I can't imagine Skye ever getting married for any reason other than love.

She might have wanted dark, filthy sex with me. The kind that allows for zero attachment, but it was clear the only reason she wanted that was that she was apparently hung up on Gabe.

I adjust my tie and then put on the most expensive jacket that I brought with me. My face is clean-shaven, and I spent time getting a haircut this afternoon to look my absolute best for tonight's dinner. I know that she chose him, but I want her to regret not having one more time with me. And I want Gabe to feel the slightest bit intimidated by me.

I pull out my phone and find the address that Skye texted me for where we are having dinner together tonight, then enter it into my Uber app.

As much as I wanted to spend the entire day with Skye, I knew that it wouldn't be a good decision. I'm not going to ruin her life by turning her into a cheater, and if I stayed a moment longer, that was exactly what would've happened. So, instead, I looked up a nearby hotel that had the nicest suite available, and I booked it. Not that Skye or Gabe will ever know where I'm staying tonight, but I'll know, and my ego is far too sensitive to not stay somewhere nice. Just because I don't typically spend this kind of money doesn't mean that I can't.

I walk out of one of the nicest hotels I've ever stayed in and over to the Uber that's waiting for me. I try not to think about what Gabe will be driving him and Skye to dinner in. Some ridiculous car I'm sure.

What I should really be worried about is how to stop thinking about Skye. Because, tonight, after dinner, I have every intention of walking out of her life forever. It's not that I care about her. I don't. But, man, do I miss her sweet ass. I miss the way her body welcomes me in, like she's been waiting for me forever. I hate how I miss the look in her eye and the sound she makes when she finally comes.

And I have to let go of the dream of ever getting to experience that again with her.

The Uber finally stops in front of the fancy seafood restaurant, and I climb out. I open the door to the restaurant that sits on a pier out over the water all by itself. The kind of restaurant that has white tablecloths at every table, at least three waitstaff per table, and nothing but the best wine on the menu.

"I'm here to meet Skye King and Gabe Cole," I say to the hostess. Names that I figured out after a quick Google search.

She sweetly smiles at me. "Right this way, Mr. Jackson."

My eyes widen a little when she says my name, but I suspect that Gabe also did the same search on me that I did on him. I follow the hostess throughout the whole restaurant to the far corner where Skye is sitting at a table in the corner, overlooking the water. She's wearing a plain gray dress that fits her nicely but isn't overly sexy. It's nothing compared to the dress she wore on the beach the night of our first date. This dress screams business. It seems more appropriate in a boardroom instead of on a date with her fiancé and her ex-lover.

I take a seat at the table, opposite Skye, while her eyes are fixed on me.

"How was your afternoon without me?" I ask.

She cocks her head to the side and pulls her hands together on top of the table. "My afternoon was quite relaxing without you."

"Good. I wouldn't want you getting your feelings mixed up about missing me, not when you have a fiancé who keeps you so completely satisfied."

She doesn't flinch or even blink at my harsh words. "You forget I could never have feelings for a dick like you."

"So, where is your fiancé, Gabe?" I ask, glancing around the room, assuming he went to the restroom or something.

Skye swallows hard and glances out the window. "He's running late. He'll be here soon."

She doesn't have to add to the end of her sentence because it's clear all over her body that she is annoyed with him for being late.

"Can I get you two a drink or an appetizer to start?" the waiter asks.

I motion to Skye, and she answers, "We will have a bottle of your house red wine and the clams to start. Thanks."

I grin as the waiter leaves to go get her bottle of wine.

"Why are you so happy all of a sudden?" she asks.

"No reason, I'm just surprised that you ordered wine. Wine means romance, and since it's not clear if your beau is ever going to show up tonight, I'm shocked that you would be willing to share a bottle of wine with me. It must mean I did something right."

The waiter returns, pouring us each a glass of wine before disappearing again.

"A lot can change in six months. I no longer think of wine as romantic," she says, taking a sip of her wine.

"Some things never change."

"So, when do I get to get rid of you?" she asks.

"I have a flight booked back home for tomorrow. So, as long as you still want me gone, you won't have to see me ever again after tonight."

"Prove it." Her eyes light up with a sparkle and gleam as she teases me to prove myself just like I asked her to prove herself earlier.

I pull out my phone, finding my plane ticket and showing it to her. "See, I have a flight booked for tomorrow. I'm a man of my word. I'll be on that flight as long as I don't discover that you lied to me. Plus, I need to be getting back to work."

"Oh, yeah, you have to get back to the dangerous world of building video games." She snickers. Another fact that I'm sure she learned when she Googled me.

"As opposed to the dangerous world of whatever Gabe does."

She grins. "Security. He risks his life every day to make sure that the richest people in the world stay alive."

"He does not. He hires men to protect his clients."

She shrugs. "Usually, but he also likes the rush of the job, so he often does security protections himself. And him working in this business puts our lives at constant risk."

I'm beginning to see what she might see in him. Because, if I know one thing about Skye, she is a risk-taker. She likes to live life on the edge a little differently than everyone else. Evidently, that's what Gabe can provide her.

Our appetizer arrives and we gobble it down while discussing all the basics that we never got around to discussing in the Bahamas. Our jobs. Why she became a veterinarian. We talk about families, about how neither of us has siblings and therefore adopted our friends as family. We talk about our favorite music. Hers is surprisingly jazz while mine is rap and hip-hop. We talk about our favorite places in the world. Hers is a small town in Italy while mine, outside of the Bahamas, is France.

We talk for over an hour as we drink our wine and order more appetizers. We talk about everything that you should talk about on a first date. We laugh, we joke, and we tease each other. And I quickly forget that Gabe might be coming. I forget that he even exists. I haven't been on a date with a woman in a long time. At least not one that wasn't just about sex.

"Sorry, I'm late." Gabe's voice rings out behind me, crushing the fantasy that we have created between us.

Skye glares at him as he leans down and kisses her quickly on the cheek before taking his seat next to her.

"Meeting run long again?" Skye asks, cocking her head to one side and giving him a look that means business.

"Yes. Had a meeting with a new client who is interested in my services. Took longer than usual to close the deal, but I did. I always do."

The waiter brings over a third glass and pours Gabe a glass.

"I'm sure the two of you had plenty to talk about while I was gone," Gabe says, looking from Skye to me.

I ignore Gabe studying Skye instead. Her reaction screams pissed. I don't know a lot about love, having never been in love myself, but I suppose you can be pissed off at the person you're desperately in love—but not for too long, or the love begins to fade. It doesn't seem like Gabe is that concerned about Skye's love for him disappearing while her anger is on full display.

He holds up his glass of wine. "I'd like to make a toast to old flings." Gabe drinks from his wine, but neither Skye nor I clink glasses with him or drink our glasses. Gabe smirks as he looks at me. "You didn't like my toast?"

"No, I didn't find it in good taste."

Gabe laughs. "I thought it might break the tension between all of us. You see, I already know about you and Skye in the Bahamas. She told me all about it the night I proposed to her. She didn't want any secrets between us," Gabe says, squeezing Skye into his body.

She pulls away, not happy to have his arms around her.

"Is that why you invited me to dinner then? You wanted to pick a fight with me for fucking your woman when she wasn't even yours."

"No, I wanted Skye to be happy. And I thought we might all be able to be friends now that everything is out in the open."

The waiter returns, breaking through the tension, and we all order our food.

"Excuse me, I need to use the restroom," Skye says, getting up from the table.

I don't know if she really has to go or if she's just trying to get away from having to deal with us.

I lean back in my chair, and Gabe does the same, each of us sizing the other one up.

"For a man who says he doesn't want to pick a fight, it sure seems like you're trying to start one."

"Let me make my intentions clear. I didn't bring you here so that you and I could become friends. I brought you here because I have a proposition for you."

I frown, not liking the sound of that one bit. "What sort of arrangement?"

"I know that you enjoyed fucking my girl in the Bahamas, and I know that you came here in hopes that you'd be able to continue fucking her. But then I threw a wrench in your plan. But I think you can help me with the problem I have. See, I want to marry Skye. I love everything about that woman, but I have needs beyond Skye. I want to have my cake and eat it, too, or so the saying goes."

"I don't understand."

"I want you to fuck Skye once a week. That will allow me to fuck my own women on the side without Skye feeling mistreated. She's a woman who deserves the best, and I plan on giving her the best. But she can also enjoy a little plaything on the side while I enjoy my own playthings."

"What makes you think Skye would agree to a plan like that?"

"She will. She wants you. Skye gets what she needs. I get what I want. And so do you. You can fuck my woman once a week as long as you understand who's in control. I have all the power. I say when this arrangement ends. If I say you don't get to touch her for a year, you don't touch her for a year, got it?"

"Yes."

"Oh, beautiful," Gabe says as Skye walks back toward the table. "That was perfect timing. Mr. Jackson and I have come to an arrangement."

She frowns, looking from Gabe to me with her eyes narrowed. "You have?"

Gabe looks at me. "We have."

"And what is the arrangement?" Skye asks.

I stand up. "That I'm going to kick his ass."

Before Gabe has a chance to react, I dive over the table, knocking him to the floor. I punch him hard in the face—one, two, three times. He basically just laughs in my face. I know that he is more skilled than me and could stop me at any time. But he doesn't. I get off another punch before the waitstaff comes over and starts pulling me off of him.

I stop mainly because I can't be here for another second. I can't let Skye be around him, either.

"What's going on?" Skye asks, pissed off as she looks from Gabe lying on the floor with blood spilling from his lip.

"I'm leaving, and you're coming with me." I hold out my hand to her, begging her to take it, and to my surprise, she does without hesitation.

I thought I came here to end things. I thought I came here to get over the fantasy of fucking her again. I lied. Because I care more than I thought.

15

___________

## SKYE

I DON'T KNOW why I took Brody's hand. I don't know why I'm going with him. I should stay with Gabe; that would make things simpler. That would be the right decision, the better choice. But it's not the choice I made.

I don't know what the hell just happened, but I have a sneaking suspicion that Gabe was the one who started it. Right now, I can't stand Gabe, and when I look at Brody, all I feel is disappointment. Both men are idiots who don't deserve me. But, right now, Brody might be the lesser of two evils.

So, I let him lead me out of the restaurant while I keep my eyes on his back, ignoring all the customers who are staring at us, shocked at the scene that we caused. I don't question him when he flags down an Uber, and we climb into the backseat.

It takes a minute for the realization of what's happening to hit me.

The car begins driving away from the restaurant before I find my voice again. "Where are we going?" I ask Brody.

Brody looks at me, and I realize I'm still holding on to his hand, but I don't dare let it go.

"My hotel."

I nod. It's what I expected him to say, but I'm not sure if it's the right answer.

I glance out the window and watch the buildings whiz by as we drive. I have no idea which hotel is Brody's or how long it'll take us to get there, but it's long enough to make me regret my decision.

"Actually, can you take me to my condo first and then drop him off? My condo is just down this street," I ask the driver.

Our driver is an older gentleman. I would guess mid-sixties. "Of course, miss."

"What are you doing?" Brody asks.

I remove my hand from his. "I'm sorry. I can't do whatever you think we're doing. I just need to go home."

Brody runs his hand through his hair, messing up his sculpted locks. "You don't have to go back with me, but you shouldn't go home with him either."

"What happened?" I ask even though I'm afraid I already know. It's going to make me pissed off. And, if I'm pissed off, I won't make smart decisions.

Brody grabs my cheeks, looking at me as he strokes my face. "Gabe is not a good man, Skye."

"What happened?" I ask again. I don't need to be told what Brody thinks of Gabe. I just need the truth.

Brody drops his hands and purses his lips as he tries to find the words to tell me the truth.

"Please."

"He wanted an arrangement where I'd get to fuck you in exchange for him getting to fuck other women. He wanted an open marriage, except it seemed he'd get the much better end of the deal. He's a little cunt, Skye. He's a bitch, a disgusting moth-erfucker who doesn't deserve another second of your time. Forget about that asshole. He's not worth your time."

I stare out the window while my hand rests on the base of it, fidgeting with the lock button. It hurts, but then I've known for a while what Gabe is.

"Skye?"

I don't answer him. I can barely breathe, let alone speak. I don't know what to do. I don't know how to get out of the horrible situation I've found myself in.

"Skye, what are you thinking?"

I can't. I just can't.

Brody senses that something is wrong. He undoes the seat belt and scoots close to me until his body is pressed against my side. He slowly moves his arms around me, pulling me into a hug. Neither of us speaks as the Uber driver drives toward my condo after Brody tells him the address. He finally stops, and I just sit for a moment in Brody's arms.

"Stay with me tonight. I have a suite, so you can have your own bedroom. I won't talk to you. I won't bother you at all. I will give you some time and distance to figure out what you want."

I nod, still unable to speak. I feel numb, rough. The driver starts driving the five blocks it takes to get to his hotel. He stops outside, and Brody, now deciding to be a perfect gentleman, opens my door and helps me out of the car. He keeps his arms wrapped around me as we walk through the lobby to the elevators. I don't remember the elevator ride, just that it happened along with what I assume was a walk to the door of his hotel room. I somehow make it inside.

"Your room is this way." Brody leads me down a small hallway to the bedroom. He goes over to the bed and pulls down the sheets, leading me over to it and setting me on the edge of the bed. Then, he takes a step back.

"Is there anything I can get you? Food? Drink? Someone to talk to?"

I shake my head.

"Okay. I'll be just down the hallway. If you need me at any time of the night, just come in and wake me."

He turns to walk out.

"Wait."

He does, exhaling as he stops.

He stares at me, and I stare at him.

Then, I stand up and walk over to him. "Thank you."

"Of course." He leans down and sharply kisses me on the forehead. And, in that second, the spell breaks.

I grab his cheeks. I move his lips to mine, and I kiss him. And, damn it, the kiss feels good.

*Why did I have to kiss him?* Now, there's no going back. There's no way I'm going to be able to stop, and it's just going to make things so much worse. It's not bad enough that I'm about to marry a crazy person, but I have to do it while being hung up with this asshole. My heart and mind are torn between two people, and I'm about to give them both what they want. *But what about what I want?*

I don't know what I want, except that I want Brody to fuck me and make me forget about everything else.

Brody grabs my neck as he kisses my lips over and over. We stumble backward until we're falling on the bed. Arms and legs tangle around each other, but our lips never part. It's almost as if neither one of us takes a second to really breathe and think about what we're doing, so we will stop. So, neither of us will allow that to happen.

Instead, we kiss, we groan, and we tear each other's clothes off. Brody rips his jacket off while I pull his tie over his head. His shirt goes next; buttons fly as it falls in a heap on the floor, showing me his hard, strong chest that I haven't been able to get out of my head since I saw him shirtless again in Albuquerque.

"I knew you wanted me the second you saw my abs again. You're a sucker for hard abs and biceps." He smirks as he flips me over and slowly starts unzipping my dress. "Did you wear this dress for him or me?"

I bite my lip, refusing to answer. If we are going to fuck, we're not going to talk about what's happening. The whole reason for sex is to make me forget, to allow me an escape, not to figure out what I really want.

He spanks me hard on the ass, and I yelp.

"Tell me who you wore the dress for, or I'll spank you again."

My lips curl up a little at that thought. I like this game. He spanks me again, and my whole body jerks at the force. My mouth waters, my nipples harden, and my panties become soaked. I forgot what it felt like to have a man be rough with me in bed. Gabe, for all his rough and controlling in real life, prefers rather vanilla sex.

"Have you had enough?" He kneels behind me, clearly getting turned on himself with every spanking as his hard cock rubs against my ass.

"No."

"Then, I'm going to enjoy punishing you until you tell me who you wore the dress for. Because I think you wore this dress, that hides your body, for me. To keep me away from your sexy body."

He rips the back of the dress in half. I flinch at the sound, knowing now that there's no way to hide what I'm doing from Gabe, not that there was before or that I would have. I'm not a cheater or a liar even if Gabe deserves to be cheated on.

"There's your body. You have been hiding it from me beneath your scrubs and this ridiculous dress but no more."

His lips brush over my ass, lightly kissing each cheek. I gasp as he grabs my legs, spreading me wide, and then his hand comes down, slapping over my cunt.

"You've been a dirty girl who deserves to be punished. Say it."

"I've been a dirty girl who deserves to be punished," I say through gritted teeth as he spanks me again.

I hear him moving his pants down, and I turn my head to get a look at his thick cock, but he grabs my hair and turns me away from him, shoving my face hard into the pillow, so I can't see anything.

"You don't get to look at me, baby. You don't get to be rewarded in any way until you answer me."

"Please."

"Are you ready to answer me?"

I groan.

"I guess that's a no." His cock pushes inside me, spreading me wide, filling me with the pain and pleasure I haven't felt in months.

"Fuck, Skye."

I feel him slip in and out of me as he pounds into my body. He slaps me hard on the ass whenever I try to look at him. And he hardly touches me, except with his dick. He punishes me over and over as he moves in and out, giving me only the tiniest bit of pleasure, driving me mad.

I feel his breath on my neck. "I know you're stubborn, Skye. And we both know how much of a dick I can be. So, answer me. Who did you wear the dress for?"

"You." I glance back at him and see the smirk on his face.

"Good girl." His hand reaches around and starts rubbing my clit as he fucks me, building me in a way that only he knows. He makes it hard for me to breathe or think about anything other than my coming climax.

He brings me close and then stops begging me with his words. "Tell me you're not going back to Gabe. Tell me you're going to break up with him."

My throat is dry, but my body still aches for relief.

"Give me a chance. I know you think I'm nothing but a dick,

but I can be so much more. I can behave. I can love you like Gabe never has."

I can't breathe. My heart aches to believe that his words are true, but I've been fooled by too many men before to believe anything that leaves his mouth, especially with his cock still inside me. He doesn't mean a word that he says.

"I won't go back to Gabe. I'll give you a chance," I say, telling my own lie.

He lets me come, and it's the relief and distraction I've been seeking, but it's over far too soon. Moments later, all I can think about are his stupid words and how I wish they were true. I think about the words that I spoke and wish that they were what I was going to do. But, right now, I can't.

16

———

**BRODY**

SHE'S GONE. I knew she would be. I knew she was lying last night when she told me that she would leave Gabe, that she would give me a chance. But I still had the tiniest bit of hope that she would still be lying in my arms when I woke up this morning. I hoped that maybe she thought of me as more than just a jerk who had treated her wrong in the past. But, clearly, she thinks I'm just as bad as Gabe—or at least, not much better.

I hear a door open, and my ears perk up. Maybe I was wrong. Maybe she's still here. I jump out of bed, not caring that I'm still naked, and run through my hotel suite, looking for her. I hear a squeal as the maid sees me butt-naked.

"I'm so sorry. No one answered the door when I knocked," she says, hiding her eyes behind her hands.

"It's okay. I'll go back to my bedroom to put some clothes on." I head back to my bedroom, pulling some sweatpants and a T-shirt on.

Damn my stupid heart for feeling anything toward Skye. I wish I could go back to not caring, not feeling anything, but I can't. She might not want to be with me, but I know that she doesn't want to be with Gabe. I don't know what power he has

143

over her. What he's bribing her with or blackmailing her with or what arrangement they might have, but I plan on figuring it out. She might have left, but I'm not going anywhere. I promised I would leave as long as she told me the truth, but she didn't keep up her end of the deal, so I don't have to keep up my end of the deal. I just have to come up with a way to make sure that she's safe. Only then can I leave her alone.

I pick up my phone, and I call Noah's number.

"Hey, asshole. Have you fucked her enough that you can come back to work now?" he answers.

"Have I recently told you that you're fired?"

"Every damn day."

"I need your help."

He sighs. "You must be really desperate if you're calling me, asking for help. I thought you handled everything yourself."

"Well, I'm up against a pro, and you're the only one I can think of with any hacking skills that might be able to give me the information that I need. I need to know everything that you can get me about Gabe Cole. Everything. Understand?"

"If she has a boyfriend, I hate to tell you there's probably not much you can do to win her back, short of just waiting it out."

"Just do it."

It takes Noah an hour, but he got me everything I wanted to know about Gabe and more. Where he grew up. When they first met. And even a strong clue as to why she's still with the bastard. And I'm planning on getting confirmation on that tonight.

I step out of the car and walk into the conference center where the charity event for Love All Animals is taking place. Skye apparently does a lot more than just run her own veterinary clinic. She also owns a foundation that focuses on connecting animals and humans in need of each other. Animals that need a home are given one by people that need a companion. I think it's the reason she puts up with Gabe.

I find my table at the back of the large space, which has a stage at the front with a large screen behind it. I paid over a thousand dollars to attend, but the money was well worth it. One, it goes to a good cause, and two, I get another chance to be near Skye.

I take my seat and ignore the others at the table, who are chatting politely to each other. I'm not here for them. I'm here for Skye.

The lights dim, and a spotlight shines on the stage as I watch Skye walk to the center with a microphone in hand. She seems happy and content. I expect to see Gabe walk up onstage with her, but he doesn't. I scan the room now and find him at a close table, watching her as intensely as I am.

She starts talking, and she commands everyone's attention in the room. Even those who were busy in conversation with others now can't keep their eyes off of her. I expected her to be wearing something professional, a dress similar to what she wore last night, but she's not. She is wearing a skintight black dress that shows off her body, her strong legs, toned arms, and just the right amount of cleavage. She looks gorgeous, and I know she's wearing the dress for me. Because, as much as I knew that she wouldn't stay in my bed this morning, she knew that I wouldn't leave her alone tonight.

"I'd like to tell you a story about the first animal that saved my life. I wish I could tell you the stories of all the animals that have saved my life over the years. Saved me from depression. Saved me from pain and heartache. Gave me hope that the world could seek good. And reminded me that we were all just animals trying to live and to survive, fighting our way through this difficult life.

"But I don't have the time, so instead, I'll share just one story about a mouse named Moe. You see, growing up, I was wild and fierce—both qualities that I loved, but my parents, not so much.

My passion for life got me in trouble many times. I skipped school and cheated on tests when I thought I didn't need to learn the material. I drank in high school and smoked marijuana between classes. I drove my car too fast. I did all the things that I know you hope your children will never do."

The crowd chuckles a little, watching her.

"But then I was hanging out with a friend who brought a mouse home to feed his snake. I couldn't stand to watch him feed the mouse to the snake, so I stole the mouse and ran. I brought that mouse home and named him Moe, and he was the best friend I'd ever had for the next year.

"I had a purpose in my life that was greater than me. I cared for the mouse, fed him, and took him to the vet when he was sick. I learned what life was really about. Fighting for others, even the tiny creatures of that we often forget about.

"After that, I found my purpose protecting all animals, all beings that walk the earth.

"Together, we've saved over one hundred thousand lives—animals and humans—and I'd like them to share a few of their stories."

The video starts with story after story of people and animals being connected, saving each other. Animals that were meant for slaughter. Dogs and cats to be euthanized because no one wanted them. Even reptiles, like lizards and snakes, were saved, all given to people who needed help. Some had mental health disorders, and others had physical diseases. Some were vets in need of animal support; others were just troubled youth, needing to find a purpose in their life again.

But, by the time the video ends, there isn't a dry eye in the house. Even I have a few tears in my eyes, even though I watched Skye most of the video.

Then, dinner is served. I bide my time before I go see her. I allow her to make her rounds and talk to everyone that she is supposed to at the event. I let her worry and wonder if I'm really here or not. And only then, when she's standing by herself, do I make my move.

She starts walking toward the restroom, and I follow her, needing a moment alone with her and knowing that this might be the only place that I can get just that. She walks into the restroom, and I step in right behind her.

A woman at the sink gives me a dirty look. "This is the woman's restroom."

"I know. I just need a moment with Skye here. It's an emergency."

Skye pauses when she hears me speak and glances over at the woman. "Could you give us a minute?"

The woman scoffs and walks out the restroom, leaving us alone. I turn behind me and lock the door, so I can have a few minutes alone with her.

She turns around and looks at me. She doesn't seem surprised at all to see me standing there. "If you think you're gonna fuck me in the restroom, then you're crazy."

I chuckle. "Never even crossed my mind." I wink.

She smiles a genuine smile, and my heart sinks.

"You're not with him because you love him, are you?"

She shakes her head.

I put my hands in my pockets to keep my hands off of her. I want to comfort her. Or fuck her in the restroom or do something to get rid of the pain hiding beneath her fake smile.

"I think I know why. It's this foundation right? He has promised to stop funding it if you don't marry him."

She looks at me without blinking. Her eyes grow dark with a fire I haven't seen sparking out of them before. "Are. You. Serious?"

I clench my teeth, trying to understand. "Yes."

She shakes her head. "You men are all the same. No, I'm not

marrying him so that he'll keep funding my foundation. I don't give a crap about his money, although it's one item on the long list of things he's tried to threaten me with."

I take a step forward, unable to resist from at least holding her in my arms.

She puts a hand up, and I stop.

"I don't need you to try to fix this. I'm not even sure that it's something that can be fixed and definitely not easily."

"Then, explain to me what's happening. Because I've tried to come up with a legitimate reason you would marry that man or even go back to him after last night, and I can't come up with any. He was the reason you were in pain in the Bahamas. He was the reason you were in pain when I saw you in Albuquerque. He's the reason your hair is tamer, your piercings are gone, and that you would even consider living in a home as fancy as his, which doesn't have an animal in sight. He's the reason for everything bad in your life, so why stay with him?"

She runs her hand through her hair. "Because he owns me."

My mouth drops. "Like, you're his slave? Like, he paid money, and you're now his property?"

She shakes her head. "No, but he might as well have. Gabe Cole is a powerful man who is used to getting whatever he wants in life. He's threatened everyone I love in my life. My best friend, the princess—he threatened her in the back of her SUV. He infiltrated her entire security team. My friend, Alicia—he kidnapped her and then filled her so full of drugs that she couldn't even remember what happened the next day. My grandmother is in a nursing home, and he stopped her oxygen twice. She barely survived. He wants complete control, and he gets that. I've tried to leave him several times before, but every time I do, he threatens someone that I love, and I just can't. Because I think he might actually kill them. Or me. And, now that you're in my life, he'll threaten to kill you. That arrangement game he was playing with you at dinner was just a test to see how much you cared about me. He was just playing with you in order to determine if he could use you as leverage against me. He would never share me."

"Have you gone to the police?"

"Of course. But he is the police. Everyone that I talked to believes his story over mine. I have no options left but to give him what he wants and figure out how to fight to get out of it later."

I can't stand it a second longer. I have to have her in my arms. And, this time, when I move to wrap my arms around her, she doesn't stop me. And I'm thankful that she lets me hold her.

"You need to leave. Go far, far away from here. He knows what happened last night, and he's not happy."

I pull back just enough to look her directly in the eyes. "I'm not leaving you. I'm not going to let him hurt you."

"He won't hurt me."

"Why? It seems like that's all he does."

"Because I agreed to marry him tomorrow."

She looks strong and defiant as she says it, like it is her choice. Maybe that's what she needs to believe, but it's her choice to save her friends and family from this evil monster. But it's a choice I won't let her make.

I look at her and softly kiss her on the lips, cherishing every moment that I have with her. Who knows when our last one together will be?

"I'm going to save you."

She doesn't argue with me, nor does she agree. Instead, she tightly wraps her arms around me and rests her head in the corner of my chest. She might not trust me, but she should. Because, despite what she might think, I'm not a dick.

## 17

## SKYE

I STARE INTO THE MIRROR, not able to accept the reflection staring back at me. My hair is dark brown and curled without a speck of blue or red or purple or any of the colors my hair usually is to make it seem bright and vibrant. My piercings are all gone. Some of the holes have even healed up. I have a simple white veil on the back of my head, and a simple white dress hugs my body.

I was never the princess. I was never the type of girl who dreamed of the big wedding with the big dress and the fancy decorations. That was never me, but I always thought that it could be a possibility. That maybe, someday, a man would care enough about me that I would want that. But getting forced into marrying a horrible, evil man was never my plan.

He was such a good man when I first met him, but how did someone so amazing turn out to be so horrible?

———

*"Your coffee is three fifty," the woman behind the bar says.*

*I nod and reach into my purse to pull out my wallet, but I don't feel it. I open my purse wide, practically sticking my head inside, searching for the wallet, but it's not there.*

*"I'm so sorry. It seems I left my wallet somewhere. Let me see if I have some cash at the bottom of my purse." I frantically dig through the purse, trying to find some money to pay the woman. I was just on on a fourteen-hour flight from Monaco to LA after visiting my best friend. I have a six-hour layover until my next flight. There is no way I'm gonna survive without coffee or food or anything.*

*"Let me pay."*

*I turn around to look at the man standing behind me. He's one of the most beautiful men I've ever seen. Dark brown eyes, a strong jaw, and muscles for days.*

*I don't usually accept money from strangers, but I'm desperate, and he is handsome.*

*"Thank you," I say far too loudly.*

*He smiles and pays the woman after ordering his own coffee.*

*"How can I thank you?" I ask as we both walk away from the coffee shop in the LAX airport.*

*"You can keep me company while I wait for my flight."*

*I smile. "I'd love to."*

———

We talked for hours. We both missed our connecting flight. He offered me a place to stay at his condo, and I accepted. I thought he was going to ask me out that night, but he didn't. He was a gentleman, perfectly nice. Not a glimmer of the monster that I know he is now.

I hear a knock on the door, and I jump.

"Sorry, I didn't mean to startle you. I just wanted let you know that it's time," Samantha, the wedding coordinator for the vineyard where we are getting married, says.

I take a deep breath and work on my fake smile as I stand up, grabbing the flowers out of the vase next to me.

"You look beautiful."

I practice my fake smile again. "Thank you."

"The bridesmaids are all lined up, ready to go down. Gabe wanted to know if you wanted one of the best men to walk you down the aisle or if you wanted to walk down alone."

"Alone." I'm very much alone, so why would I want anything different?

I follow Samantha out of the small dressing room to where the bridesmaids are standing in their cream-colored dresses, each holding a bouquet of red roses, at the doors that lead out to the vineyard. I don't know any of the women, but they all look like perfect models in their dresses. It wouldn't surprise me if there were all women who Gabe used to date or still does.

Samantha walks to the front and starts giving the bridesmaids cues to walk down the aisle. I stand at the back, eyes glossed over, trying to imagine that I'm anywhere but here.

I spent all last night, trying to come up with a plan that ended with me not having to walk down the aisle. But I came up with none. No solution or even an attempt at a solution became obvious. So, that means I'm getting married. I'll figure out a way to undo it later.

Samantha smiles at me, rightly thinking that this is the best day of my life when it's not. It's one of the worst.

"You ready?" she says, her voice chipper.

I nod, and she opens the doors.

I thought that I would smile and put on an act as I walked down the aisle to the man blackmailing me into marrying him. But, in a last-second act of defiance, I don't. I don't smile, not one tiniest bit. I look stern, solemn, like I'm walking down to my funeral instead of my wedding. I walk slowly and deliberately down the grass path lined with beautiful flowers. I don't look at

Gabe. Instead, I stare past the people standing at the end of the aisle. I look out to the beautiful vineyard in the distance. I don't even glance around at the seats to see if Brody showed up. I get to the end of the aisle and turn toward Gabe but don't look him in the eye. I continue to look past him, trying my best to pretend I'm not here. The bridesmaid behind me asks if I want her to hold my bouquet for me.

"No," I hiss.

Gabe tries to hold on to my hands. I'll marry him in front of this large crowd of people, none of whom I know, but I'm not going to make it easy for him. I'm not going to hold his hand or smile or show any happiness about it. And I won't give him pretty pictures that he can display all over the newspapers in the morning.

I glare, and he smirks back as the minister begins saying something about love and the beauty that it brings and how much better it makes everyone's lives.

I call bullshit. There is nothing beautiful about love. There was a time when I thought I loved Gabe. We connected on so many things—food, music, movies. Our bodies connected when he wrapped his arms around me, making me feel safe. The way he let me have my independence and respected that I owned my own business and had my own dreams. But it was all a lie. Love isn't real.

"I do," Gabe says, grabbing my hand and placing a ring on it before I have a chance to dissent.

"And do you, Skye, take this man to be your husband?"

"I do." I smile as I take the ring that is wrapped around my thumb and plunge it onto his finger, attempting to cause as much pain as I possibly can as I force the ring over his knuckle.

"I now pronounce you husband and wife. You may kiss the bride."

Gabe grins, but if he thinks I'm going to let him have this

epic kiss, he's crazy. He grabs my waist and back and dips me backward, away from the crowd, as his head comes down over me, but he doesn't kiss me.

He stops short and says, "You think you're so smart, defying me, don't you? But, now that you're mine, I will punish you for every act of defiance you commit."

His lips press against mine, and I bite down hard. He pulls back with a smirk. I see the tiniest drop of blood dripping down his chin.

He wipes up the blood with the back of his hand. "I'm really going to enjoy punishing you. Should I start with Alicia or Brody?"

"Leave them alone."

"Behave."

Gabe lifts us back up as the crowd cheers, thinking that we spent the whole time in a passionate kiss together instead of what really happened.

Gave interlocks his fingers with mine, firmly holding me so that there's no way for me to let go.

"Now, smile, or Brody's the first to go."

I smile as Gabe walks me down the aisle. As soon as we get back inside, I jerk my hand away from Gabe's. "Now what? How much longer do we have to do this?"

He wraps his arms around me, pulling me to his body again. "Oh, honey. This never ends. You're mine now. Tonight, we are going to spend the night dancing and drinking in front of my friends and the world, showing them just how much of an awesome couple we can be. Then, tomorrow, we get on a flight to the Bahamas to replace all those stupid memories of your old flame with me. And then, when we come back, all your stuff will be moved into my place. You'll become my full-time wife, at my beck and call whenever I need you. Understand?"

I spit in his face. "Go to hell."

I jerk free just as people start coming into the large building on the property to head into the reception area. All sorts of people I've never met start coming up to me, congratulating me, asking me how we met. Asking if I feel like the luckiest girl in the world to be married to such an amazing, rich man. But they don't really want to hear any of my answers. They just want me to smile and nod and let them talk, so that's what I do. I spend my night talking to strangers, trying to stay as far away from Gabe as I possibly can.

I reach into my cleavage and pull out my cell phone, as I take a glass of champagne from one of the waiters. Maybe if I act like I'm working on my phone, people will start leaving me alone. It works for about five minutes until I see a woman in a dark green dress and low cut neckline walk toward me.

I down my glass of champagne, needing the alcohol to get through whatever conversation is about to happen.

"Congratulations," the woman says to me in a cold voice, so different from how everyone else has congratulated me so far.

"Thanks," I say, averting my eyes elsewhere, hoping she will get the hint and leave me alone.

She eyes me up and down. "I don't understand what Gabe sees in you."

"Excuse me?"

She shakes her head. "Sorry, didn't mean to be so blunt. I'm Tonya, I used to attend college with Gabe. I thought we had a future together, but then he found you."

I sigh. I don't say that too bad she didn't succeed in her mission to keep him. That way I wouldn't be in this mess. I just stay silent.

"I just wanted to say congrats and to treat him well. And if you are ever in the need of some decorating, I'm your woman." She holds out a business card to me and I take it.

I stare at this woman completely confused at what she sees

in Gabe. She either doesn't know him well at all or likes the monster inside. Either way, I'm not about to have that conversation with her.

"Thanks, I'm going to get another drink," I say, slipping her business card and my phone back into my cleavage.

Gabe spots me from where he is boasting with his groomsmen. I slip back into the crowd to get another glass of champagne.

I drink glass after glass of champagne, and as the night progresses, I get more and more skilled at staying just out of Gabe's reach. Whenever he tries to talk to me, I push a woman in front of him, and that seems to do the trick in distracting him just long enough for me to slip further away and get lost in another crowd. But, every time he gets closer, I can feel the rage surrounding him, exuding off of him. Gabe isn't into rough sex, but I have a feeling, tonight, he is going to give a whole new meaning to rough sex. But it will be nothing like what Brody and I have done together.

"Skye, the wedding planner had a question about what you wanted to do with the leftover cake," a man who looks oddly familiar asks me. He's in a dark suit, his hair is shaved, and his eyes are bright.

I feel like I should recognize him, yet I can't place him. Maybe I met him earlier today when he helped serve me alcohol or food, although he's not dressed like a waiter.

"Excuse me," I say to the crowd around me. I follow the man out of the reception hall. He keeps walking once we get to the hallway down toward the back of the building.

"Where are we going?"

"Just a little further. Repacking the stuff into the back of the car. She wants to know what address to deliver the leftovers to."

I frown. Surely, Gabe has already thought of all of these things and handled it.

"Who are you?"

He doesn't answer immediately. Instead, he just keeps walking to the back door and pauses when he rests his hand on the door.

He smirks. "I'm here to kidnap you, of course."

I open my mouth to scream as he grabs my hand and pulls me outside. But I'm so broken at the moment that I'm not sure whether I should fight to stay or make it easier for him to kidnap me. I can't imagine anyone worse than Gabe Cole.

He pushes me into the back of an SUV, and my eyes open wide with hope.

"Brody?" I ask even though I know it's him sitting in the seat next to me. I'm still not sure I believe it's real. It must be a dream; there is no way Brody is rescuing me right now.

He grins, flashing me his perfect teeth. "We're here to save you," Brody says.

He wraps his arms around me and firmly kisses me on the lips.

"No, we are here to kidnap her. This plan will never work if Gabe doesn't think we're kidnapping her," the man who brought me out here says from the front seat.

Another man is sitting next to him and begins driving us off.

Brody rolls his eyes at him. "Fine. We are kidnapping you."

"And that means we need to make it look like a kidnapping all the time," the man says.

"Wait, you're Noah," I say, recognizing the man sitting in the passenger seat as one of Brody's friends from the Bahamas.

"Yep, and this is Levi," Noah says.

I smile at both of them. "Thank you for kidnapping me."

"Our pleasure. If you're a friend of Brody's, then you're a friend of ours. He deserves to be happy," Levi says.

My smile falters, but I don't think any of the men notice. Even if they manage to get me out of this mess with Gabe, I'm not sure Brody and I can ever be together. He might not be as bad as Gabe, but he's still a dick at the end of the day. They both even confirmed it to me in the Bahamas.

"Brody, now," Noah says.

"Sorry, but I have to tie you up. There are too many video cameras and cameras from stoplights, and Gabe could see us. We need to make it look like a real kidnapping."

I hold out my hands, and Brody's eyes sear into mine as he ties me up just like he has countless times before. I feel the familiar feelings all over my body, thinking about what is supposed to happen next. He is supposed to kiss me. Spank me. And then fuck me. It's not supposed to just end with a kidnapping.

Brody pushes his ball cap further on his head, trying to hide his face as we go through a stoplight. They are all really concerned that Gabe is monitoring us right now. And, if that's true, then none of us have a chance.

"Stop the car!" I shout.

Levi doesn't even hesitate. He just keeps driving.

"You have to stop the car. You have to let me out. He'll kill all of you for doing this."

Brody grabs my face, forcing me to look at him. He pets the side of my face, trying to calm me down. "He's not going to kill any of us. We have a plan. Just let us follow it."

I take a deep breath in and out.

"Shit," Levi says. The cars jumps forward as he speeds up, running through a red light.

"What the hell, man?" Noah says.

"We are being followed," Levi says.

"How?" Brody asks.

"I don't know. We should have had more time before anyone figured out that Skye was gone. Especially with the woman we got to play Skye. She looks exactly like her from the back; there's no way Gabe would've noticed this fast. Not when we also had one of the hottest women we could find seducing him."

"Do you have your cell phone on you?" Brody asks.

I nod and look down into my cleavage.

Brody reaches in between my breasts and pulls out my cell phone. He rolls down the window and chucks the phone outside.

"Seriously, Brody, you had one job—to make sure she didn't have her cell phone on her," Noah says.

Brody's eyes stare into mine. "I'm sorry."

Brody might be many things, but he's definitely no James Bond. I haven't even been gone five minutes, and Gabe's already on our tail. I don't have much faith that they're going to be able to figure out how to get me out of this safely. So, I'd better start forming my own plan and fast. Or we are all fucked.

18

———

**BRODY**

I FUCKED UP. And, now, my mistake might cost us our lives.

We all turn, looking at the SUV chasing after us.

"You need to just let me go. It's the only way to save your-selves," Skye says.

"No way. Not happening," I say.

Shots ring out behind us, and Levi swerves the car as all our hearts jump into our throats. Now, they're shooting at us.

"Levi, Noah, please. Just turn me over to them. Gabe won't hurt me, and you guys will have a chance to go free."

Levi grips the steering wheel hard and glances in the rearview mirror while I give him a death stare, imploring him to keep driving, no matter what.

"We aren't turning you over," Noah says.

Levi nods in agreement.

Skye exhales deeply and then looks at me. "Then, you'd better come up with something fast, or we are all dead."

I pull out my burner phone. He wants one thing. Skye. And I don't think he'd be too happy if she were dead. Or at least, I hope not.

Shots ring out again, and we all duck down like, if we get low enough, somehow, the bullets won't actually pierce our skin.

I reach into the bag at my feet and pull out the small gun inside.

"I don't think shooting back is the answer," Skye says, looking at me with wide eyes.

"Skye's right; these guys are professionals. They will shoot you dead before you even have a chance to get a shot off."

I aim the gun at Skye's had.

"I'm going to make Gabe think that we're going to kill you if he doesn't call his men off."

Skye smiles and grabs the phone out of my hand, handing it to Noah.

"Take a picture, and send it to Gabe," Skye says.

Skye closes her eyes and then opens them, trying to look as terrified as possible while I aim the gun at her head.

"You have to hold the gun closer," Noah says.

I put the gun all the way up to her head, hating how it feels to aim a gun at her, even one that has no bullets in it.

Skye looks at the gun out of the corner of her eye, and she looks terrified, just like she needs to be.

Noah takes the picture but only of my hand and Skye, giving us more time before Gabe realizes it is me who is the kidnapper.

"Message sent. Now, we wait and hope we don't die," Noah says.

I continue holding the gun to her head, hoping the guys behind us will see it and stop.

My heart races as the silence drones on, and we zip down the road, passing car after car. One second passes. Then, another. Then, another.

The phone buzzes in Noah's hand. We all hold our breath as he clicks the button to open the text message.

"He's agreed," Noah says.

We all exhale at the same time.

"They are pulling off the road," Levi says, looking in the rearview mirror.

I toss the gun back into the backpack and grab Skye's head, firmly kissing her on the forehead, thankful that she's still alive. That all of us are. But none of us are naive enough to think that we're safe, long-term.

The phone buzzes again, and Noah clicks the message open.

All of us stare intently at him, waiting for the message.

"He says that he's going to hunt us all down and kill us. But will make it long and torturous if anything happens to Skye. He wants her desperately. We aren't to hurt her. He wants us to return her to him by tomorrow morning, or he will use every-thing in his power to take us all out."

"Tell him to give us one million dollars and that we define the terms, not him. Tell him we want the money in exchange for her safe return by tomorrow evening," I say.

Noah nods and begins typing the message.

I look at Skye, who has her head cocked to the side, eyes curiously looking at me.

"It will give us enough time to work on plan C."

"Plan C?" Skye asks with a raised eyebrow.

I nod. "It takes a lot of plans, and we will go through as many plans as we need until we are all safe."

"What's plan C then?"

Noah turns around in his seat and hands the phone to Skye. She takes it with her hands still bound together.

"We need to call that rich princess friend of yours to get us a private plane to somewhere anywhere but here," Noah says.

"You can't be serious."

I nod.

She shakes her head. "First, she doesn't just have a private jet on hand at all times to take me wherever I want. Second, Gabe knows about her, he's threatened her and her family before. I'm not going to get her involved, and even if she were to get involved, Gabe would be able to track the plane in a second. If we're trying to be discreet, that's the opposite of helpful."

I rub the nape of my neck hard. "I guess we are on to plan D then."

"Actually..." Skye says, staring at the phone.

She reaches into her bra and pulls out a business card. I can't help but continue to stare at her boobs and wonder how much else she has stored in there.

She begins entering the number on the business card.

"What are you doing?" I ask.

She shakes her head and just shushes me.

"Hello, Tonya. This is Skye."

The other woman must say something, as Skye goes silent.

"You see, I know you don't like me very well. But I made a mistake, and I think you'll want to help me fix that."

A short pause.

"Because you want my husband, and I want an annulment. So, you'll help me by discreetly getting me a private plane out of the country without letting Gabe know where I am, and I'll make sure that he finds his way safely into your bed."

My mouth drops open.

"Done," Skye says, smiling. She moves and lets the phone drop to her hands before she presses End on the phone and hands it to me. "Head to the airport. We have our plane."

"How?"

"I met a woman tonight who was not too happy about me marrying Gabe. She wanted him for herself. She asked me to give her number to Gabe if he ever needed help with redecorating. But I knew it was her saying that she didn't care that we were married, that she would still try to go after him."

"We have our plane," I agree.

I'm not sure I believe that this is gonna work until we pull up at the airport, and there is the plane waiting for us. Still, I don't think it's gonna work, and we all load and carry the guns we bought as we board the plane, expecting Gabe or his men to be sitting on it, ready to ambush us the second we get on. But there is none. Apparently, a woman scorned and in love will do just about anything to have a chance at her ex-lover again.

It's not a huge plane, but it's enough for the four of us.

"Where to?" the pilot asks as he ducks his head into the main cabin of the plane.

"Vancouver," Levi says.

Skye looks at him like he's crazy. But the pilot just nods and heads back to the cockpit.

Skye takes a seat in the back, and I take the seat right next to her. "Seriously? Vancouver? Can't find a place a little further away to head to?"

I look at Levi.

"I have some friends in Vancouver who might be able to help."

I reach over and rub Skye's neck, trying to get her to relax. "I'm going to save you."

She grins. "Sure you are."

We all buckle our seat belts, and the plane takes off shortly afterward. It's only then that I realize her hands are still tied together. When we are safely in the air, I unbuckle my seat belt, and she undoes hers. I motion with her to follow me to the back. She does. We barely draw attention as Levi and Noah talk strategy in front of us.

I'm hoping there's some sort of bedroom or at least a large bathroom in the back of the plane, but there's none. Just a tiny-ass bathroom that's no bigger than a bathroom on a commercial jet. Still, I pull her inside and close the door behind us.

"Finally," she exhales as she throws her tired arms up over my head and around my neck.

Our lips crash together in a passionate kiss that beats all others. I've never needed a woman so much in my life, and it's clear she's never needed me more than now. Our tongues tangle and our breathing becomes one as our kisses dig deeper into each other's smiles. But she is still wearing her wedding dress that she got married to Gabe in.

"I'm sorry I couldn't save you before you had to marry him."

Her lips kiss me again hard. "I don't care. Marriage means nothing to me."

Her voice is sharp, like a woman scorned, not willing to get back into love again.

It's something I'll have to work on later. As desperate as she is for my body, if we survive all this, I'm not sure she'll be as desperate for a relationship with me, as I am with her.

"Fuck me, Brody. Please," she cries into my lips, her entire body begging for me but not being able to do anything about it because her hands are tied and currently locked around my neck.

I lift her dress up and push down the thin white lace panties, finding her tight cunt and pushing two fingers inside. She's soaked and ready for me to enter her in a second, so that's exactly what I do. If there's anything I've learned through this, it's that there is no promise for a tomorrow. Not even another minute or another second.

I push down my pants and pull out a condom, slipping it on just in time as she wraps her legs around me, and I push my cock inside her. I fuck her hard over and over in the tiny bathroom on a plane. Any other time, I would be reveling in the coolness of getting to fuck a woman on a private jet. Any other time, I'd be telling her to be quiet so that my friends wouldn't hear her, and I would get to keep her cries all to myself. Any other time, I would do all those things and more. But not today. Today, I'm just going to fuck her as many times as I can. Because, despite my words of promising her that I can save her, I'm not sure that I can. All I can do is fuck her and take away her pain, however temporarily.

**19**

---

## SKYE

I SHOULD BE SCARED, but I'm not. Brody has a way to make me feel safe even though he has no idea what he's doing. Even now, there is no way to save me. Not from a crazy man like Gabe. And especially not when we have no skills compared to Gabe.

I feel the light peeking into the room, and I open my eyes. All the boys are sitting around the room on their computers, typing furiously fast. We all stayed in the same hotel room last night so that we could pay with cash and hopefully make it a little bit harder for Gabe to find us. Brody and I slept on the bed. Noah, the couch. And Levi slept on the floor.

"Morning," Brody says, getting up from his computer and walking over to the bed to firmly kiss me on the lips.

The kiss makes my insides warm. I could get used to waking up to kisses like that every morning.

"This is Jeremy and Kate," Brody says, pointing to a man and woman who are also sitting in the room.

They both turn, smile at me, and nod, and then they immediately turn back, typing quickly on the computers.

"They are here to help us hack into all of Gabe's systems. If we can break in and hopefully find some hard evidence of Gabe

169

doing something illegal, we might be able to stop him. Our plan is to turn it over to journalists first, so that then when we turn it over to the police, they won't be able to deny it."

I glance around the room, but all the people are working hard on the computers. I don't know what their credentials are or how good they are with a computer. But I know their skills with a gun and car aren't great. This might actually be where they are capable of doing some damage to Gabe.

Brody eyes me up and down as I wear his T-shirt and boxer shorts. I run my hand down my bedhead, and he takes a deep breath. And then his lips kiss me again like it might be the last time. The rest of the room fades. The people, the typing, the danger. It all escapes us as hold each other.

Noah clears his throat loudly. "You need to be working, Brody. There will be time for making out later. We need all hands on deck."

Brody slowly pulls away from me. "I am working. I'm keeping Skye happy and relaxed."

"Skye is perfectly capable of taking care of herself," Noah says, still typing away on his computer.

Brody sighs and then grabs my hand, pulling me toward the bathroom. He gives me a wink as we enter the bathroom, but just as Brody is about to shut the door, Noah slams his hand hard against the door, preventing it from shutting.

"Seriously? You're not fucking in the bathroom again. You do realize we heard everything on the plane, right?"

My face blushes, but Brody just scowls.

"Get out," Brody says.

"No, you're the best programmer we have. We have a chance at saving Skye, so your ass needs to be behind a computer the rest of the day."

"He's right," Brody says, kissing me hard on the forehead again.

I close my eyes.

And then he walks out of the bathroom and back to a computer.

Noah stands at the door a second longer. "We're going to figure this out. In the meantime, here are some clothes." He reaches behind him and pulls out some jeans and a T-shirt.

"Thanks, really. Brody has some really good friends if you are willing to risk your life to help him."

Noah shrugs. "He would do the same for us."

Noah walks away, and I shut the door. I reluctantly turn the water on in the shower. My heart is torn because I don't know if I want to shower and wash away every remaining scent of Brody in my hair or all over my body. But, on the other hand, I want to wash away every touch from Gabe. But the water will calm me, and I just have to pray that I'll get another moment with Brody even if it is for the last time.

I strip and then step into the steaming hot shower, trying to push both men out of my head and just focus on what I want. I want to be alive. I want to survive to go back to the wonderful life I've created for myself. I love my life, and no man is needed to make me feel better about it.

Still, every time I close my eyes, the darkness of everything that Gabe has done creeps in. And, every time, the only thing I can do to push out those images is replace it with Brody.

I abruptly turn off the water, refusing to close my eyes again. I get dressed in the jeans and T-shirt, but both are too big for me. I applaud the guys for remembering to give me clothes at all. And then I step back out into the hotel room. Everyone continues typing and ignoring me, even Brody this time. He put headphones on to drown out the world, even me.

I walk over to Brody and lightly tap him on the shoulder. "How can I help?"

"By telling me anything and everything you can on Gabe.

Tell me some of the worst things you saw that there might be some evidence connected to," Noah answers instead.

"What type of evidence?"

"Threats against you that might have been recorded, threats against other people, money laundering, abuse, anything criminal. Start with the worst, but even something simple that could get him locked away for a few months would be a good start until we can find harder evidence on him."

I sit down on the edge of the bed, trying to think about all the horrible things that I just spent my entire shower trying to push out of my head. "Money laundering, I have no idea about, but I wouldn't put it past him. But I have no idea where to start with that. Abuse? He's never been physically abusive to me, not yet anyway. And threats, he was very careful to never put anything in writing or say anything over the phone or in any public space really beyond the occasional whisper into my ear."

"Tell me anyway. Tell us all the stories you can think of; maybe there's something you're missing."

I close my eyes and let the darkness unfold in my head. It's not that I can't remember all of the horrible things, it's that I've spent the past few months trying to forget.

"The first time I realized that he was a monster was a couple of months after we met. He asked me out. He asked to have me fully and completely. And, if I said no, he threatened the company."

"Tell me the whole story."

———

*We would meet up at the LA airport that had become our thing. Every few weeks, I would fly to LA and see him. We'd spend the entire day talking and connecting in the airport. I never left the airport, and he never asked me to. But, each time I flew out, I thought this would be the time that he would ask me on a proper date, this would be the time that we'd become more than just friends.*

*We have been talking for a while. My flight back is going to leave in less than thirty minutes. We've had another beautiful day of talking and laughing together, but it seems that this time isn't the time either.*

*Just ask him, my heart said, thumping in my chest.*

*I should. I don't know why I'm waiting for this man to make the first move when I'm fully capable of doing it myself. The worst he'll say is no or that he already has a girlfriend. I could lose him as a friend, but it's a risk I have to take.*

*I open my mouth to ask him out when he says, "Would you like to go to dinner with me tonight?"*

*I grin. "Yes."*

*I don't care about my flight or anything else I just care about having an awesome day with him.*

*Gabe leads me out of the airport, somewhere along the way interlinking fingers with mine. And that's all I can focus on—our hands linked together the entire time—as Gabe leads me into the back of the waiting car on the curb. I can't even tell you the name of the car. Just that I'm in one.*

*I'm blissfully ignorant of everything going on around me until Gabe takes the phone call. He doesn't talk much.*

*He just says in a stern voice, "Yes, it will be done." Then, he looks at me. "Small detour. I guess you'll get to know more of what I do sooner rather than later."*

*I smile, happy to learn more about his work. The car stops outside of a hotel. And Gabe helps me out, continuing to hold on to my hand. He opens the door for me to the hotel, and my mouth drops open. It's extravagant with beautiful marble floors and a high ceiling with a large chandelier overhead. Gabe rests his hand on the small of my back as he leads me toward the elevator. The doors open, and we enter. I don't know what kind of work he does that he has to meet someone in a hotel room, but I'm going along with it. That, or it's all a ruse, and he's just trying to get me naked in his bed. I think I like option B better.*

*He grabs my face and kisses me hard as my heart beats wildly in my chest. His hands go around my body, consuming me. He's definitely going with option B.*

*The doors open, and he guides me down the hallway to a hotel room where a man is standing. The man hands the key to Gabe, and he swipes it in the lock.*

*I curiously look at him as he leads me inside the room, firmly holding my hand. When we step inside, I see a man tied to a chair in the corner of the room. I gasp.*

*"Wait here," he says to me.*

*I stand frozen, not sure of what the hell's going on.*

*Gabe walks over to the man, pulls a knife out of his pocket, and slits his throat.*

*I watch the blood spill from his neck. I watch the light leave his eyes. And I'm terrified. Gabe is a monster.*

*Gabe drops the knife on the man's lap and wipes the blood that spilled onto his hands off on the man's shirt before walking back to me.*

*"I want you, and I tend to get what I want. I kill for what I want. You're mine now, Skye, for as long as I want you. For just tonight. Or for much longer."*

*He tucks a strand of my hair behind my ear. "Unfortunately, I have a flight I have to catch. More work needs to be done, and this mess needs to be cleaned up. And I know you have a trip to the Bahamas. Enjoy yourself. This might be your last week of freedom away from me." He firmly kisses me on the lips again. Then, he takes my hand and escorts me back out of the hotel room.*

*"George, take Skye to the airport and get her on the next flight back home."*

*He looks at me. "Not a word to anyone, or I'll kill you like I did to him. And I'll take all your friends and family with you."*

"I went to the police after that. They didn't believe me; they said it was all some sort of fantasy story. So, instead, I went to the Bahamas for a week and tried to forget. But, when I came back, he proposed and force me to be his. He's a monster. But he is a very careful monster. He kissed me on the elevator, so the cameras would see us, and people would assume that we went to that hotel room to have a quickie. There is no evidence."

Noah puts his hand on my shoulder and then pulls me into a hug that I desperately need right now. He's a good man, although my judgment of men is not the best. If only Brody could be as good as well. Brody's already shown me that he is capable of hurting me.

We hear a loud pop down the hallway, and everyone jumps and stares at the door. We hear a man yelling at his son, telling him not to slam the door so loudly. It was just a kid, but it was enough to get all of our hearts racing.

Noah gets up and walks over to a bag. He pulls out a gun, handing it to me. I take it from him, getting used to the heavy metal in my hand.

"You know how to use that?" he asks.

"No. Do you?"

"I know the mechanics of how it works and how to make sure that it doesn't go off when you don't want it to. But I've never fired a gun in my life."

"Same."

Noah shows me how the safety works and how to load the gun.

"Make sure it's always on you, just in case."

I nod.

I keep telling him the stories, everything I can think of, while everyone else works. Occasionally, he will go over and transfer what he feels is some important information to the others on the team to look up but after our several hours pass and they find nothing that we can use against Gabe, I start to lose hope that this will work.

Eventually, Brody walks over, and he can see the worry on my face. "We are some of the smartest people in the world when it comes to technology, we'll figure this out. But you have to make me a promise to keep fighting every chance you get. No matter what. Even if you get captured, I will find a way to save you."

"I promise," I say. But I don't think he'll be able to save me. But I can save them.

**20**

---

## BRODY

Damn it. I look at the empty bed as the morning light comes up again.

"She's gone," I say.

Noah nods. "But then we knew she would run if we couldn't save her."

"Time to move on to plan Z."

**21**

---

## SKYE

IT TOOK everything in me to leave. I snuck out in the middle of the night when everyone was asleep, passed out from exhaustion from working the entire day. But it had to be done. They spent all day searching and found nothing. No evidence to use against Gabe. They can't save me, but I can save them.

So, that's exactly what I'm doing. I stole one of the burner phones and snuck out into the night. I called Gabe and told him I'd give him everything he wanted. I'd come back to him, but he couldn't hurt anybody. He promised, and I have to return to ensure that he keeps that promise. He bought me a commercial flight early in the morning, and I got on it.

But, now, I can't seem to bring myself to get off of it. The whole plane has unloaded, except for me. Still sitting in my seat in the fifth row, I stare at the seatback in front of me. I have to get up. I have to leave. But I know, as soon as I do, my life is over. I'm as good as dead. Right now, I have to worry about saving my friends. Then, I can worry about saving myself. So, I force my body to stand. I force my legs to walk off.

"I'm surprised you had the balls to show up," Gabe says, grabbing my arm the second I depart from the gate.

On the one hand, I'm shocked that he is here instead of sending one of his men. But, on the other hand, Gabe likes to do things that are important to him in person.

"I keep my promises," I say, letting him guide me through the airport and out to his waiting car.

I'm surprised to see that he doesn't have a driver. He tosses me into the passenger seat and then climbs into the driver's seat, speeding off.

"Good girl," he says when I behave.

I look out the window instead of having to look at him. I try to remind myself that I'm doing this for them. Not for him. Not for me. No one else deserves to die for my mistake in judging men.

"Look at me."

I turn my head.

He smirks. "You really will behave now?"

I nod, keeping all the emotion off my face.

"Stop thinking about him. He's nothing. Think of me."

"I am," I say. Even though it's a lie.

I will never stop thinking about Brody. I'll never stop dreaming about him. Gabe can control a lot of things, but he can't control my thoughts or desires.

Gabe parks the car outside of our condo and then says, "Come."

I do, like a dog following a command. He leads me up to our condo. I pray that his damn phone rings with some important client who needs to be killed or secured or whatever the hell it is that he does. It doesn't ring though. We get up to the condo, and he shuts the door behind us, locking it. I know what he's going to want. I'm not sure I can give it to him. I want to protect my friends, but I also won't let him lay a hand on me. Not without a fight.

"Fix me a drink. A scotch," he says.

I walk to the kitchen and pour two glasses of scotch—one for him and one for me. I walk back to him and hand him one. He smirks when he sees the second glass. He clinks our glasses together and then drinks down my entire glass.

"Now, strip for me," he says, his eyes staring into my eyes.

I go to do what he said, but I can't. My hand stops just short of lifting the shirt over my head.

"If you hesitate, I will put all your friends' names in a bowl and pull one out. The name I do dies. And we will repeat that process until you either listen to me or they're all gone. Understand?"

"No."

He hits me hard across the face, knocking me down to the floor. I can't think. Everything hurts. My head is pounding. The dizziness overtakes all of my thoughts. I feel something hard jut into my back.

Gun. I have a gun. I reach into the back of my pants, pull out the gun, and aim it at his heart.

He laughs and rips the gun from my hand before I can react. He tosses it aside like it's nothing before I even had a chance to get a shot off. He grabs my hair and pulls me up.

"You think you're smarter than me, don't you? Better, stronger? But you aren't. You're just a stupid little bitch with a beautiful cunt that I want." He slobbers up my neck and my face when I try to push him off, but he's right. He's much stronger than I am. If he wants something, he'll just take it.

"I'm going to have my way with you over and over again. And then I'm going to do what I said; I'm going to put all your friends' and family's names in and pull one out, and that person will die today. And then I'll keep repeating until they're all gone, and when they're all gone, that's when I'll kill you."

I should be afraid, but instead, it just pisses me off. I kick him as hard as I can in the balls and run. He grabs my ankle, and I fall to the floor before I can take two steps away. I won't let him do this to me or to my friends.

We both look up as the door to the condo is pushed open. Three guys tumble in, all holding guns aimed in our general direction. But they aren't just any men. These are my men. Brody, Noah, and Levi.

I should be relieved to see them here. But I know how bad of a shot they are, and I know that, if they miss once, Gabe will kill them all.

"Run," I plead with them.

Noah looks at me like I'm the saddest thing he's ever seen while Levi and Brody both stay fixed on Gabe.

"Let her go," Brody says.

Gabe laughs. "No, she's mine. But I will enjoy killing the three of you in front of her. It will break her, and then she will be mine completely."

Brody looks down at me for just a second. I know what he's about to do. I cover my head as he shoots. I hear Gabe move behind me, pulling me toward him to use me as a shield as he reaches for his own gun. I grab on to his arm, reaching for the gun behind him with all my might, trying to keep it away from shooting Brody. I hold him off only for a second.

But then dozens of men start pouring into the condo, all with bulletproof vests and helmets. They rush over to Gabe, pulling him to his feet and disarm him.

"Gabe Cole, you are under arrest for attempted murder of Skye, Brody, Noah, Levi, and many, many more."

In complete shock, I watch as they drag Gabe out. I don't believe that this is really happening.

I turn to one of the officers. "Is this really happening? Am I safe now?"

"Yes, he won't be getting out of jail for a very, very long time. You are as safe as you can be."

"Thank you."

Brody comes over and wraps me in his arms. "I told you I would save you," Brody says.

"How? How did you convince the police?"

"I planted a recording device in the gun," Noah says.

"You were able to record our entire conversation?" I ask.

Noah nods.

"We knew you would run if we couldn't find another solution to save us. So, we used it to get the evidence that we couldn't find on our own."

"If you guys wouldn't mind, we would like to question each of you individually. That'll help build our case against Gabe," one of the police officers says.

"Sure," Brody says, slightly pulling away from me. He leans down and firmly kisses me on the forehead. "You're safe now. To live your life however you want."

He walks away, following one of the officers. And Levi does the same, following another officer out. Leaving me and Noah by ourselves in the condo.

"You okay?" Noah asks.

"I will be."

"Good. Will we be seeing more of you around Detroit now?"

I shake my head as I stare at the back of Brody's head. It could be one of the last times I ever see him. "I don't think so."

Noah watches Brody turn the corner out of the condo. "I lied. Just so you know."

"What do you mean?"

"I mean, he's not a prick. He doesn't date countless women and multiple women at the same time. He's hardly dated. And he sure as hell doesn't go around, fucking women willy-nilly. He's a nerd with a big heart. He will love you with everything he has if you let him have that chance. He won't hurt you. He's one of the good guys."

I tuck my hair behind my ear. "He's hurt me before."

Noah narrows his eyes. "You need to ask him about that."

*Is it possible that Brody is a good guy? That he won't hurt me?*

I run after Brody. "Wait!" I shout.

Brody turns around and gives me a giant smile. I run to him.

"I don't trust men. I know you don't have to guess why. My mind says I should run far away and never let anyone into my life again. But my heart wants something more. My heart thinks you might be a better man than I give you credit for. But I need to know, why did you hurt me in the Bahamas? Why did you text me a picture of you and that woman? Why did you fuck her?"

"Because you needed something to take away the pain. I never had sex with that woman. I just got her to pose with me to make you hate me. It seemed to be what you needed. Just like how you needed rough BDSM-type sex. I've never done anything like that in my life. I had no idea what I was doing. I just Googled and made it up as we went along."

I chuckle.

"I've never owned an animal. I've never wanted kids. I live a completely different life than you. We don't like the same music or the same movies or the same drinks. But I do know one thing. I love you, Skye. I love that we are different. I love that we can grow together and learn to become better people because of each other. I want to learn what it means to love animals. I want to know what it's like to have kids with you. I want to marry you and live happily ever after with you. I want everything with you."

"So, you're not a dick?"

He shakes his head.

"Or an asshole?"

He shakes his head again.

"Or a tool? A prick? A monster?"

"No. I can't promise that I'll never hurt you, but I will do everything that I can to not hurt you if you give me a chance. Will you give me that chance?"

"Yes."

**22**

---

# EPILOGUE

BRODY

"When are you coming back to Detroit?" Noah asks.

"Not for another three weeks, for the launch of our next video game," I answer into my phone.

"You know if you come back and work here, you could have a nice cushy office."

"And why would I want that? I've never wanted a nice, big cushy office." I glance around my cave in the back of Skye's veterinarian clinic. It's barely bigger than a closet. I'm pretty sure that Skye used to use it as a supplies closet before she let me make it into my office.

"I don't know, so that you would have windows and get to be with the rest of your team."

I laugh. "I hate windows and people. Seeing you every couple of weeks is plenty."

"Fine, fine. Tell Skye I said 'hi' and that she better be coming to the next launch with you."

"She is. She wouldn't miss it."

I end the call and lean back in my chair, taking a deep breath as I glance at the clock. It's six o'clock. Usually, Skye likes working late, and I do too. But it's Friday night, and one of the new vets is coming in early, so we should be able to take off soon. Plus, I have plans in store. I even spent my lunch break setting up for tonight.

I close my laptop and decide to leave it at work, rather than bring it home where I could end up working more. This weekend is all about relaxing together without work.

I look down at Grump, who is lying at my feet. "Ready to go home?"

He wags his tail and I smile, petting him on the head before standing up and walking out of my office to go convince Skye that we should go home and let the vets she hired handle the rest of the cases for today. It will be easier said than done.

I walk down the hallway toward Skye's office with Grump at my heels, following me.

I stop at the door, knocking softly, when I see that she is on the phone.

She smiles when she sees me, and I smile back, leaning against the doorframe while I look at her. She's the most beautiful woman in the world. Especially when she's doing what she loves. Her hair is currently a dark purple. Her piercings are back in her nose and half a dozen on each ear. And she just recently got a new tattoo on her hip that represents the charity that she started. She's back to who she really is, and I love watching her. I thought that after everything that happened she might live in fear, but she doesn't. She's the strongest person I know.

Grump doesn't care that she is on the phone. He walks over to her and paws at her leg until she gives him attention. She pets him lazily on the head while she talks.

I keep my distance, knowing I will have a better chance at getting her to leave if I'm patient. She talks for a few minutes longer and then ends her call.

"I still can't believe how much Grump likes you. I think he

might like you even more than I do," Skye says, giving Grump better attention now.

I shrug. "We are just a lot alike. I like my space and being alone. He's the same."

I walk over to her, wrap my hands around her neck, and kiss her firmly, letting her know that she needs to be done working. Now.

She moans a little as I kiss her. And I know if I keep kissing her, and no one comes in to interrupt us, that I can convince her to go home, where I can fuck her. We've tried fucking here before, but it never works. Her desk is too flimsy and if she's here, people are constantly coming to talk to her about a case, since she's the best.

I hear a knock on the door, and I'm about to curse whoever it is that is going to prevent me from being able to take Skye home.

"Sorry to interrupt," Alicia says with a tiny grin. She's not sorry at all.

I glare at her while still holding Skye in my arms, not letting her go for anything.

Skye laughs when she sees my expression. "What's up?"

"Jake is in surgery and could really use your help with a case. He's tried realigning the bone with pins but he just can't get it to work. Do you have a few minutes to help him?"

I roll my eyes. I've lived with Skye now for over eight months. I know that orthopedic cases like this take a lot longer than just a few minutes of her time. They take hours upon hours. If she steps in to help, she won't be home until midnight or later.

"No," I answer for her.

"Excuse me asshole? I can make my own decisions," Skye says, pulling out of my arms.

"I know you can and your answer is no."

Skye folds her arms across her chest and gives me that look

like it's going to be a long fight that I'm not going to win. I never win.

But tonight is the one night that I could really use a win. I'm not patient and I have big plans for this weekend.

Skye turns back to Alicia, a woman who I thought was my friend, but definitely isn't. "Of course, I'll help. I'll be right there."

I glare at Alicia, annoyed with her for not sticking with the plan.

Alicia starts bursting out into laughter.

"I'm sorry. Jake isn't in surgery and he doesn't need Skye's help. But watching your head explode like that was worth the teasing," Alicia says.

I frown. "Seriously? That was a joke?"

She nods.

I roll my eyes and grab Skye's arm. "Can we go home now, before Alicia decides to pull any more pranks on me?"

"Fine, grump," Skye says.

Grump's ears immediately perk up.

She laughs. "Not you," she says to the dog. "You," she says pointing at me. "You are much more of a grump than the dog."

I frown, not sure I like her new nickname for me. One, it's not practical with the dog being named that. And two, I'd much rather her call me an ass or a prick. It's much more dangerous sounding than 'grump.'

"I thought I was an ass?"

She rolls her eyes. "You're that too. But first and foremost, you're a grump."

I chase after her and scoop her up in my arms, tickling her sides as I do to make her laugh, before setting her down slowly and kissing her softly on the lips.

"You're also sweet, and romantic, and handsome, and intelligent. And mine," she says, as she opens her eyes recovering from the kiss.

"Good, now can we go?"

"Yes," she laughs.

I grab her hand and yank her hard, pulling her through the hallways and out of the building. I make sure to walk as fast as I can out of the building, so she doesn't have time to talk to anyone.

She takes her time climbing into the front seat of the pickup truck, that I'm not allowed to drive for some reason, while Grump and I climb into the passenger seat in record time. I give her an annoyed look as she slowly starts up the engine. It doesn't start at first. Instead, it makes a weird clicking sound. We live just down the road from here, but I'm afraid it's going to take hours to get home at this rate.

"Can I buy you a new car yet?"

"No, I don't need a new car. This one works fine. And when I need a new car, I'll be buying it myself."

I sigh. We've had this fight a dozen times. The first video game that we launched is exceeding our expectations and I'm earning a ridiculous salary. Skye makes more than enough money on her vet clinic. She needs a new car, but she won't spend a penny on anything until it actually breaks.

She tries to start the car again and this time it starts up. At least we aren't walking home, although at this rate, it might be faster.

She starts driving again.

"Care to go a little faster?" I ask, as I look down at the ten miles an hour reading on the dash.

She laughs. "In a hurry for something?"

"Yes, in fact."

"And what would that be?"

"I have two things in mind. One, fuck your brains out."

She grins and nods. "Of course. And two?"

"You'll have to wait and see."

She raises an eyebrow, but doesn't question me.

She has barely parked the car when I throw my door open and let Grump out. He, at least, moves quickly. Then I race to her door, throwing it open as well, and pulling her into my arms.

She squeals as I carry her inside.

"You really are in a hurry, aren't you?"

I nod, as I pull her bottom lip into my mouth. "I've struggled to work all day while I was thinking about what I would get to do with you tonight."

Her eyes darken. "What plans did you dream up this time?"

I smirk. "You'll see."

I step inside the house and immediately get swarmed by all of her pets that have somehow multiplied since I moved in. I will never admit it to her, but I do love being around all the animals. But right now they are not a priority. If I put her down, our entire night will be spent giving them attention and I'll never get her back.

She sees the look in my eyes and wraps her arms around my neck as she starts kissing me again. "Fuck me. I want to know what mischievous thing you have in mind."

I kiss her lips, shutting her up, as I head to the bedroom. When I get inside, I kick the door shut keeping our pets out, so that I can have Skye all to myself.

I watch as Skye's eyes widen when she looks around the room at the rose petals around the room and the swing attached to the closet doorframe.

"What's this?"

"A new toy."

"And the rose petals?"

"I thought we could mix a little romance with our dirty sex."

She grins.

I don't wait for her to ask more questions or figure out anything more about what's going on. I grab the hem of her shirt and lift it over her head. She shimmies out of her scrubs and my eyes burn into her black lace panties and bra that she wore beneath her scrubs just for me.

"Like what you see?"

"Love."

She bites her lip and blushes. She does every time that I use the word love. She's about to blush a lot more tonight.

I push her body against the door, where the swing is and kiss down her neck, loving the taste of her skin. She smells like heaven when I kiss her. A mix of sweat, lavender, and sex.

She eyes the swing behind her with a nervous glance. "Have you tested this out to make sure that we don't break my door?"

I bite her bottom lip to shut her up from asking stupid questions. Then I lift her body up, slip each of her legs into the swing, and then tie her hands up at the top so that she can't move.

Her eyes go up to her hands and then down to me.

"Did you want me to test it out first?" I ask, knowing that she really didn't. She loves the thrill and excitement. Of course, I made sure that she wouldn't break the door, but she doesn't need to know that. She's a thrill seeker that lives for this.

I don't let her answer the question. Instead, my lips push aside the lace covering her pussy and I lick her clit, then slide into her already dripping pussy.

Her body clenches around me as her moans fill the room.

"God, I love your pussy."

I watch, as she struggles against the restraints in the swing. I love watching her body spread wide for me.

I take a step back and remove my shirt, loving the look she gives me when she sees my shirtless body. I take my time removing my jeans and boxer briefs. At least, I attempt to move as slowly as I can. Usually, I can be patient; take my time and really savor her. Not tonight.

Tonight, I need to make her mine.

I walk back to her and loop my finger between her panties and skin and rip them to pieces.

"You owe me new panties."

I smirk. "It was worth it," I growl.

I grab her hips, as my cock hardens at just the sight of her naked pussy. My cock rests at her entrance as our lips collide and I push inside her. She feels tight and slick and welcoming. She moans, as I thrust in and out of her.

"Harder," she moans.

I do. She may be tied up and unable to move, but she still has control, even if she doesn't think she does.

I fuck her harder and harder, her body easy to move in the swing. Her eyes roll back in her head, and she bites her lip harder before she screams my name.

I come inside of her, filling her with my cum.

"That was amazing," she says with tired breath.

I grin. "You like that?"

She nods.

"Now help me down."

I hold up one finger as I slip out of her and walk over and pick up my boxer briefs. I slip them and my jeans back on before I walk back to her.

"Down. Now."

I grin and cock my head to one side. "And why would I do that?"

She frowns. "Fuck me again or help me down. You're not leaving me like this."

I sigh and help her remove her legs from the swing, leaving her arms tied.

"And now my arms."

I take a deep breath and then kneel down in front of her.

"What are you doing?" she asks, sounding annoyed.

I reach into my back pocket and pull out a small box. "I'm proposing."

She snickers. "You are not proposing with me still naked and tied up."

"I am too, it's the only way you will let me propose."

She frowns.

"Now...Skye, I love you with everything I have. I've wanted to marry you since the first time I fucked you. I know I've screwed up and that you deserve better, but let me spend eternity making it up to you. Marry me?"

Her eyes widen.

"No."

I sigh. I knew this would be a fight. It's why I proposed with her tied up.

I stand back up. "No? I thought you loved me?"

"I do."

"Then why won't you marry me?"

"Because I don't want to."

"That's not a reason."

"Because technically, I'm still married to Gabe."

I roll my eyes. "He's in prison and you can easily get that annulled. That's not the problem. What's the real reason?"

She sighs. "I don't want to get married, ever."

"Why?"

"Marriage doesn't mean anything. I married Gabe and you saw how well that worked out."

"That's because he coerced you."

"And what are you doing?"

"Asking, very persuasively."

She frowns. "I'm not a normal woman. I don't want normal things. I don't need kids, I'm happy with my pets. I don't need a husband, I'm happy with my partner. Why can't you get that?"

I run my hand through my hair. "I can. You're right. I shouldn't pressure you."

I walk over and place the box on the nightstand and then I start walking to the bedroom door. I open it and start walking out.

"You can't leave me like this!"

"I'll be back when I'm ready to fuck you again." I've left her tied up plenty of times before. It only makes the next round better.

"Wait!"

I stop. Is she going to use her safe word? She hasn't the entire time I've been with her and I've pushed her limits pretty far.

I turn around and walk back into the bedroom, standing in the doorway and loving looking at her standing naked.

"Why is marriage so important to you?"

I think for a moment. "Because it's getting married to you. I love you. I want every experience possible with you. I want the world to know that over all the other assholes in the world, for some reason, you chose me. I want to call you my wife. I want to celebrate you with all of our friends. I want to marry you because I love you."

She sucks in a deep breath, and I think maybe, she might change her mind. Maybe, she'll say yes.

"You're a dick."

I smirk. *Wrong as usual.*

She opens her mouth again and her lips curl up into a grin. "But I love you. I want to spend the rest of my life with you. And if you want to get married then...yes, I'll marry you."

I grin and run back over to her, kissing her firmly on the lips.

"And I'm not saying yes because you tied me up and forced me to talk to you about it."

I laugh and undo the ties on her wrists, releasing her.

She wraps her arms around my neck as she eyes the box on the nightstand. "And if that is a diamond ring, I'm not wearing it."

I shake my head. "Well, open it."

She lets go of my neck and walks over to the box and opens it. She takes the piece of paper out and begins to unfold it.

"What is it?"

"I didn't think you were much of a diamonds person, so this is a picture of a tattoo that I got designed that I figured we could both tattoo on our bodies in lieu of wearing a ring."

She stares down at the picture a tattoo that represents everything she is. Fierce, loving, and strong.

"I love it."

"I love you."

I kiss her again.

"You're still an ass, you know."

I grin. "I know. And tomorrow I'll be a prick, or a romantic, or a jerk, or whatever you want to call me. But I'll always be a man that loves you."

The End

Thank you so much for reading *Heart of a Prick*! If you want to receive updates on when the next book is coming and get my **FREE** book, **Not Sorry,** signup here: ellamiles.com/freebooks

Read more in the **Unforgivable** standalone series here:
Heart of a Thief
Heart of a Liar

# ABOUT THE AUTHOR

Ella Miles writes steamy romance with a twist. She's currently living her own happily ever after near the Rocky Mountains with her high school sweetheart husband. Her heart is also taken by her goofy four year old black lab that is scared of everything, including her own shadow.

Ella is a USA Today Bestselling author, author of the Amazon top 100 bestselling books: TOO MUCH & SAVAGE LOVE, and Kindle Press author. She is also the author of the ALIGNED series, MAYBE series, DEFINITELY series, UNFORGIVABLE series, and NOT SORRY.

*Stalk me at:*
www.ellamiles.com
ella@ellamiles.com

# ALSO BY ELLA MILES

Too Much

Aligned: The Complete Series

The Maybe Series

The Definitely Series

Not Sorry

Heart of a Thief

Heart of a Liar

Dirty Obsession